MOUNT APPETITE

BILL GASTON

MOUNT APPETITE

RAINCOAST BOOKS

Vancouver

Polestar Books and Raincoast Books gratefully acknowledge the support of the Government of Canada through the Book Publishing Industry Development Program, the Canada Council and the Department of Canadian Heritage. We also acknowledge the assistance of the Province of British Columbia through the British Columbia Arts Council.

Edited by Lynn Henry
Text design by Ingrid Paulson

National Library of Canada Cataloguing in Publication Data

Gaston, Bill, 1953-
    Mount Appetite

    ISBN 1-55192-451-X

    I. Title.
PS8563.A76M68 2002   C813'.54   C2001-911684-5
PR9199.3.G373M68 2002

Library of Congress Catalogue Number: 2002102366

At Raincoast Books we are committed to protecting the environment and to the responsible use of natural resources. We are acting on this commitment by working with suppliers and printers to phase out our use of paper produced from ancient forest. This book is one step towards that goal. It is printed on 100% ancient-forest-free paper (100% post-consumer recycled), processed chlorine- and acid-free, and supplied by New Leaf Paper. It is printed with vegetable-based inks. For further information, visit our website at www.raincoast.com. We are working with Markets Initiative (www.oldgrowthfree.com) on this project.

Raincoast Books   In the United States:
9050 Shaughnessy Street   Publishers Group West
Vancouver, British Columbia   1700 Fourth Street
Canada, V6P 6E5   Berkeley, California
www.raincoast.com   94710

1 2 3 4 5 6 7 8 9 10

Printed and bound in Canada by Friesens

For Edythe

CONTENTS

WHERE IT COMES FROM, WHERE IT GOES

NOT KNOWING WHAT WAS afoot in the next room, Mr. Oates told her to stand and take off her blouse. He himself removed the bra straps from her shoulders, carefully so that nothing more fell. It did sometimes make women nervous, this laying their skin bare to him, for they knew he was no official doctor. At the same time they seemed to understand that exposure, that some kind of intimacy, was part of this. To him the clothing didn't matter. It didn't get in the way of his work unless it was distracting, like a fluffy sweater, or that scratchy metallic material, like woven Christmas tinsel — lamé? He'd had them all under his hands. Just like he'd had a few women reveal slinky underthings, black or shameless crimson, and these women had an attitude to match, as if seducing him would get them more from him, or win some of the Gift for themselves to take home. Well, he would say unto those women, Get thee gone.

Standing and facing her, Mr. Oates put his hands on the old shoulders and closed his eyes.

"Okay, den," he whispered, more to himself than to her. "Let's see what ya have dere."

He'd seen from his glance out the round window that it had begun snowing. Soon would begin the season of bad backs from shovelling walks and slippery ice, people he had a mind just to send to the chiropractor in Edmunston. But that was arrogant.

All were welcome, like this old woman whose body he could feel wasn't as close to death's door as her eyes had suggested. But she was welcome.

Mr. Oates did his deep breath and long exhalation that tailed, as it should, into the emptiness that grew, and turned into a hollowness, a hole into which something must now flow. It was hunger in the shape of his whole body, and yes, into him came tidings of this old woman's pain, first an aching deep mid-back that he could tell never left her. He could also feel the early black whisperings of her eventual death, it felt like distant nuts being cracked, but that was still far off, and anyway it was something that could not be taken, at least not by him. This ache behind her stomach or liver he could probably take. Perhaps he already had, for he could feel it strongly.

Mr. Oates could smell the old woman now, rotten fruit. It was time to finish and move on. She had been in too much pain to bathe, he understood this, but he wanted her to leave. What he did took only seconds to happen or to not happen, but they often had a look of small panic if he took his hands away after what they believed was too short a time. As if one of God's minutes wasn't as good as two, as if miracles had to do with time.

"Mudder, t'anks for comin'."

He had taken to calling all women "mother." He didn't know why, other than at first it had thrilled him and now it just felt good. Even for young girls. Little mothers, something nice in that thought. If it made him more mysterious, there was nothing wrong with mystery.

The old woman — a LeClair from Plaster Rock — put her bra straps up but kept her blouse off, as if she might ask him to have another go. She stood still, staring hard at nothing, looking within. She flexed her shoulders, testing. Then shyly twisted her torso, one way and the other, and though Mr. Oates never cared to know if it had worked or not, and looked away as she moved, he was content to have seen her smile rise, lifting the wrinkles in her face.

"Did you sign the form?" he asked, and she nodded yes. "If someone's out waitin' please send 'em in." Carefully not changing his voice in the slightest, he added, as always, "If you would like to show yer t'anks, dere's a shoebox by the door."

HE WAS NEVER CERTAIN HE HAD DONE ANY GOOD, DESPITE what was said about him. Usually the only sign that he did well came in the amount of money in the shoebox. Sometimes they left little, sometimes they left a lot. But it didn't really have anything to do with what he did or didn't do. The people around the Restigouche, families he knew, as a rule didn't pay much. They were poor, why should they? And their eggs or ham or offers to plough his drive came in handy. But those who had made a journey generally left the most. Which actually meant they were more bursting with hope. You couldn't blame them. The locals came with headaches and rashes but the folks from away were often dying. Educated people, who knew medical names for their diseases. They came regularly from Montreal now, and Bangor and Saint John and Halifax of course, and when he tested his memory he could count on his fingers Boston, Toronto, New York City, Baltimore, then the scatter of real foreigners. The two Germans last month, both skinny with AIDS and holding hands — he hadn't changed their condition one bit, he didn't think, but they left a small fortune, in German Marks they were called, and which

Annette had said the Plaster Rock bank couldn't take and had to send up to Edmunston before they'd change them and put money into his account. But nine hundred dollars. If there were many more like those two, soon he would have his building.

THE LECLAIR WOMAN GOT HER BLOUSE ON AND WENT OUT, the floor creaking with her weight. Mr. Oates sat down. The trailer shuddered when she stepped, closed the door. He could not tell if she had paused at the shoebox. God bless her.

In twenty years he would be as old as the LeClair woman and he was already tired. The Gift didn't always tire him, though sometimes, as now, it felt like a great burden on his body and, if he let it, on his spirit. But in these six years since the Father and His Son and Mary had left him with the Gift he knew how close it was to sin even to let himself feel his fatigue.

But when he was tired, like now, he felt closer to the shabby ground. He could feel in his bones how spring still hadn't come. He could smell mildew in the grey rug, which had to be fifteen years old. The floor of this old mobile creaked almost anywhere you put a foot down and the room he worked in was damn ridiculous. Annette's old bedroom, it was baby-sized. The small round window, which had been someone's idea of a desirable added feature, looked ridiculous too, even with that crystal dangling in it. The window never got sun and the crystal was wasted there.

So much needed to be better. His own eyeglasses were old-fashioned, and he had heard there was a new kind of lens you could get that made thick ones like his much thinner. There'd be nothing wrong with a decent haircut once in a while. You don't want to look attractive but you don't want to be unattractive either. You don't want to be a smoothie but nor do you want to be a clown with bottle-bottoms for eyeglasses. Folks thought he was strange already, why add to the picture?

Mr. Oates stood, took a normal deep breath, then touched his toes. He stretched up and touched the ceiling, which he could just barely do. The time had almost come to spend his money. A shrine to the holy Gift he had been given. He would buy a cleared acre on the lee side of a hill closer to Plaster Rock. He would get in a wide, wide lawn like the First Baptist had, buy a small tractor with a mowing tool. Gather the unearthed boulders at the lawn's middle and paint them white.

Maybe it should be nearer Edmunston itself so people could find him easier. No more orange arrows nailed to trees at corners of dirt roads. He would live in enough comfort so he wouldn't be this tired, and so would Annette, in her own bedroom instead of the couch, and she should have a car, one with four-wheel drive. There would be nothing wrong with getting himself a skidoo — though that might signal to the folks that he was willing to do house calls, which he was not. He would keep the same humble shoebox for donations, with its sign on the lid he'd lettered in green marker: GENEROSITY IS THE VIRTUE THAT PRODUCES PEACE. When he'd read these words in a book an early patient had given him, he'd instantly seen them to be true and liked them for his box, even though donations to God's Gift had more to do with thanks than with generosity, as such.

He sighed as he rose to greet the next one. He could hear the heavy footsteps of a man, clunky and self-conscious, probably an embarrassed farmer with cancer or emphysema whose wife had forced him to come. As the door opened to reveal an untidy man in overalls whose bejeesus liver bulged in plain sight of even mortal eyes, Mr. Oates decided to give more thought to the idea he had for the building — it felt Roman, or Biblical — of two stone waiting rooms, with that marble panelling, one for women and one for men, with a bath, a jacuzzi bath, in each, so that they could cleanse themselves before coming in. And they would enter unto him in freshly laundered robes. Not the hospital kind but good bathrobes, either terrycloth or that velour.

THE FATHER, HIS SON AND MARY HAD GIVEN THEIR GIFT during a vigil of love at four in the morning with Annette, his daughter and only child, who was in the feverish last stages of what they said was a leukemia, though from the start there were doubts what it was. The look in her eyes that night had made Mr. Oates see her as a young child, eyes so full of fear and hope and trust that her daddy could make life right. It was like she had *become* a baby again, her only chance being to start over, could she please be a baby once more and have another try. Oates could not help but take her up and hold her tight. When his crying lessened and his own fatigue left him emptier than he'd ever been before, he took a slow deep breath, he didn't know why. When he let it out there was a feeling left inside of less than nothing, a cool hunger, a hollowness that invited all. Into him rushed Annette's fever and the horrible wrong in her blood, sour pinpricks by the thousands, it felt like every cell in her body flashed once for him, a sky of prickly fireflies within, then all was dark and warm. Mr. Oates felt close to vomiting up this feeling, this completion, which felt like his daughter's good red flesh, but he didn't.

Perhaps only seconds had passed. He knew something had

happened. Perhaps she had died in his arms. He kissed the top of her head and pulled away to look upon her. Annette was breathing steadily. She slept all night and in the morning she was hungry for the first time in weeks, and so beautiful to see that neighbours came in to stare at her getting better.

Word was slow to spread. There was only Annette, who couldn't remember her cure. He himself wasn't one to talk. But neighbours could not help wondering at her health. After Mr. Oates' shy descriptions of his loving hug, though no one used the word "miracle," perhaps they made the story colourful when telling it, for an odd young Moncton woman with perhaps twenty earrings visited and asked if he'd seen an angel, or if candles had lit by themselves. No, he said, he'd simply hugged her, but a special hug and something had happened.

A month later a desperate woman, Mary Niles, one of the Edmunston Nileses, brought her baby to Mr. Oates and asked him, simply: please try.

AFTER THE FARMER WITH THE DYING LIVER LEFT, HE SAT tiredly. It was his sleep time, his two to three o'clock break, there was a sign to that effect in the waiting room. But he thought he heard a foot shuffle. He waited for someone to knock but no one did. He sat for perhaps five minutes, too tired to sleep, watching, through the silly window, a harsh snow falling. He decided he wanted to take a breath of that air and he stood up quickly and opened his door. There was young Scott Nevers putting the lid back on the shoebox. A handful of bills lay beside it on the table. Mr. Oates stared at Scott and Scott stared back.

"*What?*"

"I —"

"Take 'er!" Mr. Oates yelled.

"Dey —"

"Take 'er 'n' GO!"

"But dey —"

"GO!"

"But dey said."

Scott Nevers closed his eyes and started blubbering. He was sixteen or so but still had baby fat and there was something wrong with him upstairs. Mr. Oates had seen younger children cuff him with disdain. Scott's word "they" had alerted Mr. Oates and made him not quick to chase the thief.

"Who is 'dey'. What did 'dey' say. Stop cryin', Scott."

"Dey said it was, dey said it was okay."

"Scott, stop cryin'. Who is 'dey'?"

"Dey said if you caught me you'd curse me. Please don't —"

"*Who is dey.*"

"My, my dad. An' Mr. Renous, an' *everyone.* Dey *all* said."

"Why would all of 'em say it's okay dat you steal my money dere, eh Scott?"

"Dey said you don't care. It's always been like dat."

"You mean you stolen from me before?"

The look Scott Nevers gave him was surprised and then stupidly sly in a way that said much.

"Who ya take the money to dere, Scott?"

"I dunno."

Mr. Oates hit him only the once.

"Who ya take it to. Stop cryin'."

"It's, it's Mr. Renous divvies it out."

"Divvies — ?"

"He says it's everybody's and you don' mind."

Mr. Oates touched the lid, reading the little sign, all finger-smudged now, GENEROSITY IS THE VIRTUE THAT PRODUCES PEACE. He lifted it off. Inside there looked to be a like amount of bills as the little stack on the table.

"What, you take about half, dere, Scott?"

"Best as I can get 'er, Mr. Oates." Fooled by Mr. Oates' tone, he looked ready to smile. "There's the cheques to count up, I gotta leave them, so —"

"GET OUT."

Scott looked quickly down at the money, confused about whether he could or couldn't still take it.

"OUT."

"Please don't curse me —"

"OUT!"

MR. OATES POUNDED BACK INTO THE HEALING ROOM AND stood breathing hard. *Damn them.* He looked around quickly, almost panicking at the gritty carpet, the miserly window, the mismatched chairs, the clown-and-balloon wallpaper he'd put up when Annette was born. He had only half the money he rightfully should have. His bank account in Plaster Rock, which he pictured as a red thermometer like the United Way used on the City Hall lawn, should be twice as tall. He squinted recalling the new skidoo he'd seen Paul Renous riding this winter, he was almost certain it was Renous on that, a model he'd never seen before.

Mr. Oates shook his head in a spasm, as if something obscene had fallen onto the skin of his face and he must fling it off. He found a chair with his hand, and sat.

Paul Renous, his evil eyebrows that met in the middle, his sideburns almost to his chin, his facial tics — jumps of skin in places you wouldn't think were muscles. Could Mr. Oates afford to fight Paul Renous again? It had been years ago. Renous with his cousin dying of cancer, the police, Renous' lawyer from the city acting like *he'd* killed her for christsakes. He'd made no promises, he never made promises. Mr. Oates had had to secure his own lawyer, whom he hadn't liked either, who'd helped only because he was getting richly paid to. The case was eventually thrown out of court, no thanks to the lawyer, whose only usefulness had been to write up the waiver sheet for people to sign, *I the undersigned understand that this is not a medical procedure and that Mr. Arden Oates makes no claims to be in any way …*

This time it meant *him* going to the police. But it would be impossible. He wouldn't be able to tell them how much had been taken. He could see their eyes as he explained what he did to earn his money.

His door was ajar and someone rapped timidly on it.

Trying to keep his voice steady, he said, "Gi' me two minute, den come in."

He sat straighter to still himself. If the Gift took effort on his part it was in finding the quiet inside. He couldn't be thinking wildly, or hard. Putting his hands on his knees, he took a few practice breaths. There had been only one other like Paul Renous. Her eyes dark and accusing, that woman from Cape Breton who had cut out her own tongue, whose husband had brought her, who knows why, how could you restore a tongue? Her mouth was shaped like a complaint. Maybe the desire had been for Mr. Oates to cure her spirit, an evil attitude that had caused her to do that to herself, and stare at him with such accusation, smiling cruelly at him as he put his hands on her shoulders and took his good breath.

He stared at the wall and the wall only, casting aside memories of this woman and images of his shoebox, of Scott Nevers creeping up on it every week, or every *day*, how often did they come and rob him? How did Renous "divvy it up," how many people took it, how many people along the Restigouche were robbing him blind and riding *his* new cars and snowmobiles and living in *his* buildings? *He would himself appear unto the rabble, he would speak their names and shame them, and they could make restitution according to their shame.*

She was in the room and halfway to him before he saw her, a skinny young woman with glasses thicker even than his. When he looked up at her she stopped and stood.

"Where you from, den, mudder."

"Lachine. Lachine, Quebec. There's so much pollution there, they say that's —"

"Dat's fine. I don' need to know."

She was pale and sickly. Cloudy in the brain, or stupid too. Her eyes went quickly to this and that for no reason and she didn't see any of it. She wore a long-sleeve T-shirt and he saw no need to touch her skin.

"Stand right dere mudder and jus' relax."

He approached and put his hands on her shoulders. He took a few breaths. Then the big one, which he released slowly, till there was nothing.

No hollow feeling arrived. Mr. Oates waited a second. As if a baseball were about to be pitched to him, he shifted his feet and waggled his shoulders. It didn't always happen the first time. He took the deep breath once more, and let it out, trying hard to go deeper. Nothing.

"What wrong with you, mudder?" It was a source of pride that he rarely had to ask this.

"The environmental disease. It means I'm allergic to almost everything." She smiled nervously. "First they said it was all in my head, then I almost died."

Copying the knowing voice of a mechanic lifting a hood, Mr. Oates said, "So let's have a look den."

He breathed deeply, trying again. Then again, and then once more, but he made no connection that he could feel. The woman stood calmly through it. For all she knew this was what he did and maybe now she was cured.

Mr. Oates tried once more before turning from her. He couldn't remember a less fruitful time with anyone.

"Dat's it."

"Well, thank you." She stood where she was, unsure, smiling hopefully. "So that's it? I mean, should I come back? I could stay overnight somewhere and —"

"No, dat's it. I hope you feel better. Maybe come back in six months if you want to. But I don' tink so, I don't tink you will."

"Where do I pay?" She was smiling so hard. You could see her dreams rising like bubbles.

"Dere's —"

He stopped himself. In that instant of speaking he thought he felt where it had all come from, and where it had gone.

"If you would like to show yer t'anks, dere's a shoebox outside the door."

THE ANGELS'
SHARE

HUMBLED BY MANY KINDS of hunger, Evelyn beaches her father's old kayak. In darkness, she struggles out, getting wet to the knees. Her legs already weak and frigid from this long day, the cold water feels cruel, a well of possible sickness.

Dragging, she lifts the bow high so not to bang it on rocks she can't see. She feels with her shoes, softly crushing barnacles. They are alive but this doesn't nudge her. She knows their cool, scrambled-egg insides — twice now she has tried, and failed, to eat some.

Up in sand past the high tide mark she drops the boat, finds a log, sits and catches her breath. She shuts her eyes hard to steep them in more total darkness, give herself the vision of a cat. She will be stringing her tarp by feel.

She has doubled back to this shoreline campground she passed an hour ago. It was a decision her body made on its own, her arms suddenly stroking backwards, starting the kayak's slow turn — her body's need for other bodies tonight, for their campfires, voices.

She whispers, "herd mammal," and opens her eyes.

AT THE BUTTRESSING ROOTS OF A CEDAR SHE FINDS A GOOD flat spot. A bat swoops a welcome, or a warning. She is tired of reading signs: it's a bat. Her last tin of sardines and single rice cake she eats standing in the dark. Eating food you can't see could be depressing, but tonight it's entertaining, fingers tooling in flesh and oil. It's like she's fueling up for a party.

Murmurs and pot-clatter come from random distances. Lanterns are scattered thinly about. Somewhere, a young child cries. A girl, she thinks. Overtired. The bend of her whining lament she can feel in her own body's memory, the whimper, I want to be home, I don't want to be here, *make it all stop*. Sleep is the only answer. Now part of Evelyn wants to lie down, roll herself up. Fall into the forest's safety. These huge park trees, safe from loggers and standing confident for that. She could lie dreamless at their feet. But she has to dispose of this sardine tin, bait for raccoons. She needs to move the blood in her legs. When the moment of decision comes, she knows she will check out that fire nearest the beach. You herd mammal, you.

EVELYN SEES THEM REGISTER HER HELPLESS CLOTHES, HER grey-streaked hair. Notes their appraisal: she is alone at a time of life when she shouldn't be. She is careful to sit apart, for she smells. Hellos and small talk — in the fire-circle everyone is automatically friendly.

Fatigue like hers makes hallucinogenic the chiaroscuro of firelight on faces. She tries not to stare as she gleans:

Francis and Shelley are approaching goofy with their red wine, celebrating their bookstore's closing, another casualty, they say, to the Chapters chain. Turning failure into adventure, they are leasing a shop in Gastown, to sell candles and curios, maybe New Age books in a corner nook. Otherwise almost pretty, Shelley has a willful growth, a sort of mole, riding the outside of her nostril: it's the size and shape and colour of a baked bean.

Then, Jack and Jean, from Chicago, mid-forties — Evelyn's age, in any case — are on an easy, paunchy cycle through the Islands. She imagines them chatting and taking in the smell of pine, the squirrel husking a nut. They sit shoulder-to-shoulder, waiting for someone to say something funny, whereupon they both laugh generously. Their laughter has a Chicago near-drawl.

Then Jordan, maybe twenty. He sits across from her so she sees him through dips of flame. He softly fingers a guitar, with occasional crystalline notes, trying for the best background music he can, in service to them. Shelley has asked him where Bree is, or maybe it was Free, and Jordan says, *In the tent being alone.* He smiles but looks sad saying it.

Francis and Shelley have their wine, Jack and Jean six of those fruity coolers, Jordan a wineskin on a cord. Evelyn declines when Francis lifts the wine to her and apologizes naughtily that they are drinking straight from the bottle.

When asked about her own journey, Evelyn tries not to sound evasive, difficult when she has no answers, not even to keep to herself. She doesn't mention her mode of travel. Nor does she tell them that, other than the ghost two days ago, they are the first people she has spoken to in a week. She ends up saying next to nothing. Camping, one is allowed brevity. She tells them she is on walkabout. Francis and Shelley nod, Jack and Jean laugh like she has told a joke, and she hears Jordan's fingers shift into something softer for her. Evelyn likes their company. They are past small talk, and describe for each other what they see in the fire, agreeing how the cedar, compared to the alder, breaks down into patterns of rectangles. Shelley, her dark bean not at all ugly, announces her self-amazed discovery that Haida art must have been born of staring at burning cedar.

Someone mentions Eden. From where they sit they can see nothing but a flashing buoy. More sea monsters out there than lights, Evelyn says. She adds that she imagines them calm. Jack and Jean laugh at this. Evelyn is hungry already and wonders if tomorrow she will be easy enough with any of them to ask for food. Or if she will have to steal it.

THEY HEAR SOMEONE PROUDLY PERCUSSIVE ON THE BEACH gravel. A man arrives out of the darkness, swinging a full bottle.

"Here comes the whiskey," is how he announces himself, but Evelyn sees him more articulately announced by the others: Jack and Jean glance at each other, Francis whispers "not again," and Shelley's face gives up, muscles gone, a social death. Her bean looks ugly again. Jordan begins playing louder.

He sits next to her on the log. Late forties, he has a new untended beard, wire-rim glasses, a bookish quality and a smile that never drops.

"*Peter* Gore," he says to her, offering his hand, proper as can be. He has an English accent and speaks with exaggerated stresses.

"Evelyn."

He is looking at the others, smiling. They, too, appear to be waiting.

"Okay," Gore says. "After last *night*, which still *hurts*, I expect you to *help* me with this." He waggles the bottle. "This is *too* much to ask of *one man*."

He has clear plastic cups. Evelyn alone accepts some — it is good Irish. Gore happily glugs it into her cup until she thinks to say stop.

"This *thing* in the *paper* today. *My* my." He shakes his head, pausing so someone can ask him to continue, though no one does.

"This fellow in *Vancouver*? Was spotted walking in a *park*, missing one of his *feet*. Fresh stump, blood pouring out, walking on the *bone*. Just walking. Out for a *stroll*."

After a sip, Evelyn holds the cup to her eyes and watches the firelight through it. The light is alive — the colour of a hunting cougar. Peter Gore is easy to suss. Travelling alone, he can't stay alone, and he can't let talk fall below the colourful.

"At a park *bench* they found the *foot*, and the *ax*." Gore waits again. "Can you *imagine*?"

No one can. Gore goes on to wonder how solid the delusions of the insane must get. He dismisses as pedestrian the "*voices* telling me to kill my *family*" stories, and lists his favourites, including a man who "electric drilled his head, numerous *times*; *when* was he satisfied?" — another a man who sewed a chicken — "the *saran*-wrapped kind, the standard *chicken*" — onto his belly, then went about his life until it began to rot on him and he was discovered.

"How solid is *that*?" Peter shakes his head as he drinks. The cup doesn't move with his mouth and whiskey trickles in his beard.

Jordan plays chords now — "Proud Mary," it sounds like. Peter smiles quickly at everyone in turn. He waits a polite time, then turns to Jack and Jean.

"Where you biking *tomorrow*?"

"We thought we'd go up to Quadra Island," Jack says. He turns to Jean and nods with her.

"*Wow* now that is a *long* long haul. You are *properly* ambitious."

"By bus," says Jean. She places her empty in a brown paper bag and folds its mouth up tight, suggesting they will now leave the fire.

"It takes bikes," explains Jack. "There's a rack on the front end."

Evelyn doubts she will ever grow so solid that she will sew a chicken to herself. But since Peter Gore arrived she has a too solid sense of the night around them. An empty pressure at her back, she feels the cold truth of eternity — countered here by the tiny inferno of their fire, which keeps them unafraid. Huddled early humans, drawn to a fire's heart while not necessarily liking each other. Why else are they sitting here? Why else is she at this campground? Her voyage having no solid direction other than *away*.

"*You're* giving the angels their share." Gore is speaking to her.

"I'm what?"

"The *angels'* share."

"The angels share?"

"Of *course* they do."

Gore grins at what they learn is his pun. He explains "the angels' share," an Irish notion about alcohol that is allowed to evaporate.

"As in *cooking*. As in good whiskey that gets *ignored*." Gore points to her cup and laughs, but not sarcastically.

Spirit to the spirits, Evelyn thinks. She pictures her father as a spirit. One with little practice at it yet.

Peter Gore takes a break from his noise to lean back for a glance straight up. Doing so he reminds Evelyn of a boy, a hopeful boy who has no clue what is in store. His glance, almost a salute, is so humble a look that Evelyn realizes Peter Gore is kind.

Gore looks up again, smiles and takes an outsized sniff.

"Ahh — ya hafta stop," he says in American, "and grab them roses."

No one save Evelyn laughs. She knows his joke included the thorns. She downs her whiskey, and asks Peter for more. And more, when he fills it only a quarter full.

"*I'm* sorry," says Gore. "But did you just call me a *mammal*?"

SHE CAN QUIET A MAN LIKE THIS. HE WANTS ONLY ENTER-tainment. He lacks eyes to see what's in the fire: faces hideous or godlike or mirroring any possible mood. He can't hear the tiny marimba of pebbles in waves, or the silence that is their aching measure. Can't parse the accents of smoke, or smell the beach as a charnel ground of clams, the non-stop enormity of this. He is handicapped in ways that invite anger. He needs only distraction, like any boy. She could sleep with him, but won't. Another possible mood. Or maybe if she drinks down this heft of whiskey.

"I want to show you something really cool," she says, to Gore alone. He turns to her, his mouth slightly open. It is pleasing to make him quiet already. What she's done affects everyone. Jordan's hand falters in its strumming. The fire crackles loudly. It's as if someone has offered a wedding cake to the barking dog; someone has invited the clown to come with them into the bathroom. It is pleasing, too, while watching him gather his whiskey and get clumsily up (why is it the English rise so clumsily when nervous?) to know that the others have no grasp of her now, none, and only see two gargoyles pairing off.

"Come on." She steps into darkness, toward water. "Lots of rocks. If you're drunk, hold on to my sweater."

"*Wait* then. Maybe *you* should hold on to *mine*."

"I'm not drunk."

"Then you're a *spooky* little thing now *aren't* you."

THE LAST TIME SHE CAMPED WITH HER FATHER, SHE WAS twelve. Dad fished; she gathered. Their final day, a van pulled into the site beside theirs with a family of three — father, mother, son about Evie's age. The boy glanced her way furtively, once. She was taken by their silent activity. The father, red-faced, structured their camp in minutes: cooler, containers, cleansers, lined up on picnic table. The mother untied a rake from the van's roof and cleared twigs. The boy shook out, then re-folded, sleeping bags. Then mother set up two chairs, sat alertly in one and opened a book, tucking her bookmark in her shirt pocket. The boy, with no curiosity about the world around him, sat with his book and pocketed his bookmark too.

Evelyn understood once the father began his chopping. Neither mother nor son watched him as he stretched, touched his toes, then took from his back pocket two white gloves. From a stiffly tied bundle he unwrapped an ax.

"Check the gloves?" Evie's dad whispered to her, smiling, watching too. Beer on Dad's careless breath.

Evie saw her own site for the first time — its scatter of dishes and kindling, her cairns of shells. A sloppy × against the tent, Dad's two fishing poles were still baited with ragged, dry herring.

The white-gloved father chopped and stacked firewood while the other two read. Then, as the three gathered tensely to commence a hike — the father de-gloving and wrapping his ax, mother and son bookmarking then standing — Evie saw that being out in the wilderness meant you had to reinvent how you did things. She also saw that their way was more insane than hers.

Three decades later, as she foot-feels through wilderness with Peter Gore, Evelyn remembers freedom's invitation. She can invent herself. In fact she must — every moment, here she is. No matter what new facet of honesty, or ruse, she will be surprised by her own unfolding.

"WELL," SAYS PETER, KNEELING, FINGERTIPS VIOLENTLY tickling the water, "I've never *seen* this."

Evelyn stands beside him, smelling the sea, its brew of ice and vegetation. She docsn't remember why phosphorescence comes out in certain places on certain nights. She does know it is alive, some kind of plankton that gleams when moved, hence the comet-trail behind a paddle or a hand. As a child, one night while her father cleaned fish on the dock, she saw a seal or something streak past, a ten-foot flash. She can hardly imagine the wake of a killer whale. Or a still bigger whale, passing below her kayak, the sea becoming a sun.

"I know a good one." She taps his shoulder. "You're the man. You bring that." She points to a white, skull-sized boulder.

Beside them, barely visible, a rock bluff rises from the beach. Evelyn begins to climb. She hears Gore unearth the boulder and huff.

"*Kaboosh*," she calls back, her only explanation.

"I'll follow you anywhere," he says. She enjoys his timing. "You little *spook*."

She is drunk enough to take extra care. They climb the twenty feet to the top and settle sitting side-by-side. Behind them they can just make out the campfire, but hear no voices. Peter points out a ship, a cruise ship judging from the tiny stacked strings of lights.

"Alaska," she guesses.

"Look how *bright* it is," says Peter, who's caught his breath. "Imagine the *noise*." He stares. He winds up. "Platters of *crab louie*. *Show* girls. They're packed into a great bloody *stereo*." He sounds genuinely sad. "You can see the goddamn *conga* line … grey heads *cuing* up, all smiley and *daring* …"

She hears a clink on the rock as Peter opens his whiskey. Somehow this superb Englishman has ascended with a boulder and a bottle both. A proper alcoholic. She accepts another drink, though she shouldn't. She lacks water for a thirst late in the night.

"It's Ellen, right?"

"Evelyn." She loves that he's comfortable with having forgotten. He's asked her none of the usual. His selfishness is pure and harmless. He's a man she could tell everything to.

"I'm writing a travel book on the area," Peter announces. It's all he says. It's as though he's reminding himself. She can hear doubt in his silence.

"Will I be in it?"

He does a cockney, "Depends, dunnit?" and she imagines the wicked smile. He takes a noisy gulp.

Evelyn moves to stand. "We should get this rock in the water." The climb down will get harder with each sip. "Give it a heave."

"No no. You do the honours. I insist."

She takes the boulder in both hands. Together they edge toward the brink. In front of her she can see nothing. Neither rocks nor water. The phosphorescence will be good.

Suddenly he steps behind her, scaring her. She feels him slide two fingers into her empty belt loops. He pulls her back, anchoring her against him. She can feel the bottle he has tucked down the front of his shirt.

"How's that?"

In answer she brings the boulder to chest level. She pauses, taking it all in. In front of her: absolutely nothing.

Into it she heaves the rock. Her lurch surprises Peter Gore and she easily takes him with her, over the edge. She grazes something on the way down and then they hit the water hard. The sea freezes, is bright with churning fire. Evelyn flails, yells through clenched teeth. She has no clue where to swim until she sees a light — the campfire, not the ship. She hopes Peter can swim.

They are on the beach and only seconds have passed.

"*Jesus!*" Gore is striding in a circle. "*What just happened?*"

"I hurt my leg."

"You — you *jumped*. You pulled me *in*."

She has worked her hand under her canvas shorts. Up on her hip she can feel the cut, and the blood more slippery than water.

"Could have *killed* us." He circumnavigates her, crunching gravel. "You're *mad*. I'm *leaving*."

"Wait. I hurt my leg."

"That was *insane*."

Stinging salt lets her feel it perfectly. The cut is long and narrow.

"*Why did you do that*?"

"You'll wake people up."

Peter Gore stomps off, hissing to himself. She thinks he is leaving, but hears him double back. To get at the wound, she begins to wiggle out of her shorts.

"Okay, so is it *broken*? Can you *move* it?"

She remembers the boulder pulling her with it. Or maybe she followed. She recalls a feeling of no resistance. She hadn't jumped. She'd done exactly nothing.

"I didn't jump."

"Right. Can you move it?"

"It's only cut."

She is out of her shorts and he is kneeling beside her, rigid with anger. Her underwear gleams white. She wonders if it's alive with phosphorescence.

"I *think* I can see it. It's black. Is it right here?" He touches near the cut.

"Yes."

"Can you walk then?"

"I think I'll just relax here." She smiles, speaks carefully. "It's such a nice night."

"*Oh* , but you're quite the spook."

"Peter?"

"What."

"Do you have your whiskey?"

"*Jesus*."

She hears him remove his bottle from his shirt, open it and drink. He holds it to her hand.

"No. Could you pour some in the cut?"

She hears him hiss something about "bloody western movie" as burning liquid splashes onto her hip and pelvis. The glugs become gligs and the bottle is empty.

"Right. I'm *out* of booze. Are you coming along?"

"No. Thanks. You go. I'll hang out here a while."

"Fine."

"Good night."

Gore crunches off and she can't hear him once he reaches the grass.

SILENCE IS IMMEDIATELY THE BIGGEST THING. SHE LIES still, breathing softly into it. She can hear her breath and, when she tries, her blood's steady rush. The pain of the whiskey, sharper than the salt, pins her to the sand, focuses the night. Pain the sharpest facet.

In no time at all she finds that her mind has wandered. To tomorrow's paddling — can she? — and now again to her father. His death, vast and confused, was nothing like this. She is simply lying on a beach with a pain the size of a small bright carrot. Still, the night grows so much wider for it. Her breath stops at an understanding: *away* will expand the more she paddles into it. And then: a pain like this can distract her from such notions. With a finger, she flicks the cut, freshening it.

THE MOON IS UP AND SHE IS COLD. SHE SHOULD GET TO her blanket and tarp. Her cut spikes when she shifts. She picks up her head to see. Her gash has clotted. Her legs are splayed.

Underwear stained with blood and liquor, body covered in smudge. A waft of alcohol catches her nose. She lets her head fall back.

Footsteps on the beach. They are soft, and remain soft, until they are just above her, when they stop. It could be Peter, trying not to wake her. She pictures Jordan, the guitar player. She senses curiosity, and a kindness. It could be anyone. How she must look, sprawled so rough under the moon. She knows that, whoever it is, he can smell the whiskey rising from her and she feels generous with this entertainment.

THE ALCOHOLIST

LYLE VAN LUVEN TYPICALLY GOT into these arguments with his employers. And typically he kept a civil tongue, simply explaining himself as he had so often before. Which over the years hadn't gotten any easier — how to explain colour to the blind?

"I am not a brewmaster," van Luven began, choosing *via negativa*, "nor am I a chemist. Nor am I a slave to Bavarian Purity Laws."

Again he raised the ostentatious silver mug, smelled the navïeté of its contents, put it gently down. A pain gripped his abdomen and he put his hand to the desk-top, quickly but gracefully, for support. He was explaining himself to someone named Peter Philips, owner of Vancouver Brews, another venture into the microbrewery industry. This West Coast was, apparently, still flowering with new afficionados of beer, those ready to dismiss the chemistry of Molsons or Labatts in favour of anything whose label read "hand-crafted in small batches."

Van Luven stood in Philips' new office, which smelled of its peach-tinted paint, so he would not stay long. One wall was a window onto the brew operations below; another afforded a moneyed view of the North Shore mountains. Van Luven had been warned of heavy corporate backing here. He could see with his own eyes that beer was not Philips' primary love.

"Mr. Philips, if you want this wheat beer of yours, this blond, to be 'the best in the city' —"

"Country."

" 'Country.' Then you'll have to introduce a less conspicuous, more subtly engaging —"

"Okay. Good. What?"

Philips had no time for intimacy with his beer. He wanted it whizzing off the shelves.

"It must be subtle."

"Yes. Fine. What?"

Van Luven had no stomach for further debate on the difference between "mass appeal" and "quality," how they were very nearly mutually exclusive, and how a business approach refused to consider this. In his younger days he would have lectured. That time in Toronto he had pointed at the belching distillery and shouted at them all, "*This should be your church!*"

"That's not for me to say yet. We'll be involving the nuance of four, maybe five, partial flavours. So — I'll ask you again." Van Luven paused in punishment. "How is it — exactly — that you want your customers to *feel*?"

DURING THE CIRCUITOUS FERRY TRIP TO HIS PENDER ISLAND home, Van Luven reread favourite bits of the Buddhist tantric text he was studying, those passages on *prajna* and *alayavijnaya* which both calmed and energized him for the way they described the workings of his ordinary genius. He suspected the current beer project might be his last. While his death had no exact timetable, the growing fatigue and pain would soon demand a decision from him. The Vancouver test-batches would be ready in two weeks. He sensed the best route would be to tone down the apricot hints, which promoted a cheap kind of acidic *fun*, in favour of a more bodied, after-nose of smoky oak. This would be eccentric in a blond, but all save the most deadened drinker would gain from it a homey warmth and confidence. Actually, they would gain this whether they were aware of it or not. There was a suitable hops coming out of eastern Oregon.

After Vancouver Brews, van Luven had invitations to work with a distillery in Los Angeles (pollution there making his throat constrict at the notion), and with a vineyard in, of all places, France. *Estates de Petit Rhone* had asked that, if he came, he keep his visit a secret. While van Luven's reputation in Europe was solid enough, there remained that Old World embarrassment over employing a North American taster. All of which piqued van Luven's vanity, of course, and he considered going. He suspected their problems lay in the relationship of rainfall and fertilizer. El Nino muddied age-old habits. They'd had a scientist in and now they knew, as van Luven always had, that this was beyond science. But the job was some months away, which might be too late.

THE EXTREME LOW TIDE, COUPLED WITH THE HEAT OF THE day, offered a waft of percolating mud-and-seaweed that smelled deeply vital. It felt nutritious just to inhale. Well, it was. In any case it was the perfect tide to bag kelp for his garden, and he would have done so were it not for, again, the matter of time. He stood on his narrow porch surveying his vegetables, and the equation arose unbidden: how much more food would he be needing? This question broke down into smaller equations: If

I fertilize with kelp today, will I still be alive when the garden reaps the benefits? How many more meals will I want to make of that chard? Why not trade half of that garlic for more of Oswald's carrots?

Since they'd resolved their fight last year, his elderly neighbour Oswald had been almost aggressively generous. The fight had centered around carrots. Van Luven had traded some green onions and romaine for a box of Oswald's carrots, one bite of which informed van Luven of at least two chemicals that would make him mentally ill for days. Oswald caught him burying the carrots on the beach. After assuaging the older man's feelings, a long discussion about organic gardening ensued — van Luven didn't bother going into much of his own history, or talent, except to say that he had finely honed senses — and Oswald was won over. For two years since he'd been eager for van Luven to try out his organic this and that, which van Luven did, having to bury only about half of it, mostly root crops, which continued to absorb the soil's residual nonsense.

Oswald was fine as far as neighbours went. They often stood and chatted at the spot between their two properties where a fence would have been. And van Luven loved — loved — old Oswald's cat, an unnamed stray tabby. The cat seemed to like van Luven too, and at his approach was given to a display of coy and ribald that looked almost like humour, something van Luven could not recall ever seeing in a cat.

VAN LUVEN TOOK HIS STEAMING DINNER OF NEW POTATOES, chard and parsley onto the deck, to eat standing up. He didn't like so spartan a plate, but he was out of the Saltspring lamb, the only meat he still enjoyed. For a decade, the salmon here-abouts had been losing their elan, giving him only their encroaching lethargy. Tomorrow he would phone and order a hind quarter. He would like another few meals of lamb. The innocence of their romp.

To his right, van Luven could feel the pampered growth of his garden; to his left, on the rock outcrop, the quieter swellings of moss and lichen, which sucked their life out of deadfall and, astoundingly, granite. The otter family should be cruising past within the hour. He admired their enactment of an ideal human family — two parents and three children — in the way the parents led and coaxed and herded, and the way the loopy pups splashed and played disappearing games in the kelp. They no doubt suffered crude neuroses and various otter problems, but van Luven couldn't see them.

He turned to take in his empty plate, stopping to stare at his reflection in the glass door — was his skin yellower, or was that the sun? — then at the glass door itself, which needed clean-ing with vinegar. He eyed the missing cedar shake above his head, its gap-toothed look of poverty. It was natural that of late he'd been stopping like this to stare at and chastise his house, and his land. Easiest was this assessment of place, comforts, life-scat. Easier than taking stock of his accrued *being* — which inevitably led to the house-of-mirrors taking stock of that which was taking stock.

The heavy look of the house was Shirley's doing: post-and-beam, thick cedar siding, a house to withstand earthquakes and two centuries of weather. They'd built it as their summer retreat, though van Luven, certain he could never again live in any city, secretly knew it would be his home. Shirley, his third wife, now third ex-wife, was a professor of engineering. Her world was one of physical equations. They had seemed a good match, for his world was also one of equations. But while hers could be explained, his could not. His influences on the house, for instance, could be seen in the six Balinese wind chimes (the diamond sound of which cured some of his more rooted depressions) hanging at strategic windows, and the uniform white curtains with their lemon trim. The undoing of their marriage had less to do with his insistence on bare stone floors than on his inability to explain himself. "Allergies" worked for a time, but the word grew thin, and was in any case a lie. In the end, him saying that "the spirit of manufactured tile makes me minutely insane" simply *sounded* insane. Nor could he explain how he knew that his sensitivity to the world was growing.

But it had always been thus. It had been a surprise to learn he was different from other children. Whereas other kids joshed while munching two and three hotdogs, his one bite gave him the dumb fear of the slaughterhouse, visceral knowledge of a mix of mushed parts congealing in a tube. Not to mention an instant salt headache. Tropical fruits awarded him exotic moods he otherwise wouldn't have known. Sugar was a harsh and wonderful drug.

One straw that broke Shirley's back was otherwise funny, and she had laughed without mockery. Nostalgic one day, trying to better remember details of his childhood, van Luven had made himself a peanut butter and jam sandwich, wrapped it in wax paper, put it in a paper bag, let it sit unrefrigerated for five hours — then took it out and smelled it and became instantly eight.

When he met Shirley, van Luven hadn't yet developed the liver cancer, nor what they now said was a tumour in his brain, but he was well into his cirrhosis. In this he hadn't been forthright. He hadn't been able to explain to his first two wives his love of alcohol, and why he "couldn't just spit the wine out" at tastings, so why had he thought it would be any different with Shirley? He'd tried. Alcohol, he told her, is not just alcohol. The alcohol in one beer is not the alcohol in another. Alcohol was not framed by ingredients, it was made by them. What was the yeast eating as it died, expelling its vital poison? What was its environment, what was its *mood*? These were questions more spiritual than scientific. More, what was the relationship of the alcohol to the human body? This affair was *not* consummated on the tongue. No, the only bed of this romance was found deep, deep in the body.

Harder still to explain was that, just as the truth of Calvados — good God, it was *called* 'spirit' — was discernible only in front of a rustic fire, at dusk, in something akin to a hunting lodge, so the truth in a German beer was available only to those who knew to chug the earthy froth down, exhaling noises of satisfied aggression as you clunked the thick mug on a table, which would be made of wood.

He couldn't explain, but his proximity to spirit spoke for itself. It had earned him his money and modest fame. Almost anyone could feel in themselves the difference between three drinks of draft beer and three drinks of scotch. But how many could feel — *feel* — the difference in a Pinot from one valley and a Pinot from the next? Or the difference between 1985 Laphroig and its 1986 sister? How many would know it's been stored months in a decanter? That had been washed with detergent? Or if this ice cube was made from spring water? Not on the tongue, but in their being? How many people *became* the trace of detergent, or the spring water, or the patient corpse of peat in the scotch?

Addiction was an equation too. In truth, a marriage. And disease its necessary divorce.

VAN LUVEN WASHED HIS PLATE AND FORK, AND CAME BACK onto the deck to watch the otters. Hit with a sudden bad pain — the one that penetrated front to back and effectively bisected his body — he sank to the deck floor and put his knees up. He took several deep, rough breaths. Some of the pain he still could manage to feel as "interesting," but most now he could not. The small you could own; the large owned you. Knees up, keep the moans low and steady, releasing. He had his heroin coming, at great expense, promised from a friend of a friend of Shirley's. (He repeated to himself the funny phrase — "shipment of heroin" — which sounded like bad television.) He'd been assured that if taken through the nose it would be enough for weeks of pain. Or if taken all at once, to end things. He'd read De Quincy and others, and wondered how it would be, entering opium's palace. How long would he stay, before the millions of angelic candles extinguished themselves?

He had tried for a time to let his senses seek out a route of miraculous healing. He'd eaten certain vegetables and herbs, and even leaves and grasses, tasting and feeling in these the birth and fresh workings of new tissue — it was for the most part a raw, giddy affair, precipitous in its balance between the toxic and the vital, and one that felt nauseatingly like his own gestation. Nor did it work. The playground scamper of new cells did little but bounce off a densely scarred and tumoured liver that felt more mulish than stupid in its determination to die.

Hardest to explain — and doctors would be the first to laugh at this — was his certainty that his cirrhosis was caused not so much by alcohol but by imperfect intentions, and by ignorance. Insecticides. Additives. Actually, the real poison taken in during his life of alcohol was the greed, the *lack* of spirit, of those who made it. This he could taste. This he had absorbed.

The pain lessened enough for him to doze. These days he was always tired, but he could sleep only when pain let him.

HE AWOKE TO THE SQUEAK AND BANG OF OSWALD'S SCREEN door. He decided to stay down for a while, though he might miss the otters. This light rain on the face was pleasant, though he wished also for music. In recent years he'd been exploring music's visit to certain of his tissues. He didn't have a medical image of where sounds located themselves, but time and again certain tones gravitated to certain spots in his body, elbows and kidneys and ribs in particular, and he could hear the sounds in these new ears and feel them influence how he felt about the world.

But now not even his wind chimes could keep him awake.

COLOURS OF SUNSET TOLD HIM HE'D SLEPT AN HOUR OR TWO. He got to all fours, then stood. The pain had settled enough for him to walk the beach. The odd yellow in the sky — was it real, or was there bilirubin in the fluid of his eye? Was that possible?

Van Luven stepped carefully in his sandals; some rocks were slippery, others were armed with collars of barnacles on which he'd often cut his toes. Walking, he studied the shifting planes of light coming off sand, off rocks wet and dry, off seaweed in all its curves, colours changing even as he watched them. It was true you never saw the same place twice.

He paused at the lip of the tide, facing out, his sandaled toes half in the icy water. To his left, in a patch of clean sand, was a scatter of prints where his otters must have emerged, a rare event. He could see in the prints' patternlessness their nosing and dashing about. Curiosity, whimsy. He'd missed it. Maybe they'd left the water because he wasn't looming at them from his deck. He could see lines where their tails had briefly dragged; children's tails, adult's tails. Tales.

Vancouver Brews. Should he try to give Peter Philips the best blond beer in the country? Should he give him a good beer at all? Despite his wayward day, some part of him had been at work and had arrived at a deep, beet-like nuance, followed by layered aromas dissolving by turns — salmonberry, honey, faint leathers — to the oak finish. It would look blond but hardly taste it. It would have blond's effervescence yet something weighty and generous; a beer to dispel many an off-mood. But why should Peter Philips have it?

As if beckoned, van Luven turned to see a full moon rising over the mainland mountains, and it startled him with meaning. It looked, it felt, like completion. Without much thought on the matter, but some surprise, he knew it would be tonight.

He had never had much fear of death. Death was simple, surely: if there was nothing, he would not know it. If there was something, it would probably be much like now, for there was no reason for it not to be.

Tonight. How? He had painkillers enough. If there was a way to keep from vomiting … He literally could not stomach … If there was a way to exit with senses open, uninjured …

It was a medium-sized oyster, perfect, and for no reason other than that he picked it up, spied a suitable rock, and dashed it down. A quarter shell broke off, enough for him to get a finger in. The flesh was sun-warmed. Not constricted by the bite of ice or of lemon, its taste was grandly oyster. He knew that his tasting so fully the creature's flesh was all the thanks it needed.

Spinning on his heel, carrying the empty shell, van Luven understood that life could end on a note of humour. The whimsy of an otter. He traced his steps back to the otter family's scamper-ground and knelt there, studying. He pitched forward momentarily, dropping his forehead to the sand. It seemed he'd passed out, for moments only, a new thing.

But there, an otter pup's perfect paw print. He admired it for a moment, its heart-warming symmetry. Then eased the shell-edge into the sand, pushing gently, scooping the entire print intact. He stood and held it to his face — a paw print in a shell. This he would send to Peter Philips. He would include instructions that it be added to the initial vat, and that it would linger in spirit in all brews to come. He would suggest a label depicting nothing but a closed oyster shell — which was none other than a sealed promise — and that there should be no words on the label. A man like Peter Philips might even do such a thing. And it might even work. The beer might actually taste good. There were stranger things than this.

Van Luven stared possessively at his paw print. He would add — one thing more. The edge of shell was as sharp as it needed to be and, an interesting pain, he cut himself deeply on the thumb pad. One drop, two, three, onto the paw-print sand, black dots spreading in.

Now van Luven jerked back in surprise at himself. Here was something he had not properly tasted. With caution, and respect, he lifted his thumb, bringing it to his tongue. In the instant of taste, he knew what he would do.

Softly licking his lips, he steadied his hunger. Taking shallow breaths, he rose in courage, muscle. He took a deeper breath, held it, and under the rising full moon the shell sank deeply into his wrist.

He didn't have to suck, he had only to receive the rush, to swallow in suckling rhythm to his heart beat. His continuous stream. In its taste, the truth of a mirror. The hot bronze of all he'd known. Van Luven went easily to the sand, the river of himself leaving no room for any more effort, or thought.

DRIVING UNDER THE INFLUENCE

H E LEFT THE DAVY JONES IN a hurry but stopped to stand beside his car, fingers hooking the door handle. Because this night was one he wouldn't forget, behind him the common droning bar-noise stood out poignant and fresh. He stared up past the leaves and streetlights into the overhead dark, where you couldn't see anything, not a thing, not even proper black. He shook his head, then self-consciously shook it again. He could smell the heaviness of the summer and the tide. The season was over-ripe, and starting its downslope, its rot.

Spatula gave an impatient yelp from behind the window, his black nose sticking out, snuffling in the two-inch gap he'd left so the old guy could breathe. Stupid nose poking out like that could almost make you smile.

With all the windows open it was loud as he drove the water-front route, passing all the rich houses, a good half of them with security company signs planted at the head of their driveway, these the first and sometimes sole impression you got of the house, and what kind of social gesture is that? He kept his right hand on the neck of his dog, who'd just spent hours alone yet was only content to have him back. Spatula sitting up on the passenger seat, happy as he ever got, panting while watching the human world go by.

The general waft of tepid tidal night was broken by pockets of cooler air, and he didn't think he was imagining that such air gave him a clearer picture of what had just happened, of how things ended back at Davy Jones. Patrice with her bare arms and shoulders, simply turning away from him, already talking, like he was gone and had never been.

Seeking fresher air he made a sudden left at the lights, heading uphill. By now Patrice would be talking to Steve, who would have side-stepped his way over to her table before the empty chair had cooled. Steve had always had a snaky side, you could feel him waiting in the wings. Or maybe it would be that boring Danish guy who'd started drinking there, Carl. Probably Karl with a K. In any case there was no sense wondering when he would see her again. The fight hadn't taken many words this time. Patrice with her shoulders — he felt like a simple dog for liking her skin so much, and for liking it shown in public, but he couldn't help it, he'd never been able to help any of it. Patrice would be smiling already, maybe trading one-liners, yucks about her lousy lovelife, maybe even about him. Well, you couldn't begrudge her a laugh.

Steve or Karl. He wondered what it would be like to fight either one. Not much, probably. And a fight would be the last nail for her. No, they'd just pounded their last nail, a fight would be an extra. A fight would be an ornament, red flowers on the grave. Karl, his bland, open face, almost an invitation. Did they fight in Denmark? You couldn't imagine from looking at Karl that he'd ever put a guy down, or had his face on cement himself, the grit and scrape that lasted weeks and was the worst part about it.

Up on the crest of the hill, damn, a road-block, a spot-check. Strategically placed, no way to turn off without a car chase. Two cruisers, four cops, two on either side of the road. They wore orange Day-Glo vests and swung long, headbanging flashlights. He wriggled his ass in the seat. There was no avoiding this. If he blew his parole, he blew his parole, but Jesus, c'mon. He shook his head, a fierce spasm to flick away any sloppiness, any loose-cannon nerves. He wasn't too bad. How many? Six? Eight? Way over the limit, sure, but as long as he wasn't made to blow he'd be fine. The windows open, there'd be no carful of breath. He murmured to Spatula, Here we go.

He slowed and braked behind the two cars ahead. A big cop wrote on a clipboard as a female cop leaned in to shine her light at a driver. She asked a question, got an answer, swung her light, turned her attention on the next car to come. His mind was blank. There was no use rehearsing, and now it was his turn.

He crept ahead and braked where she flagged. Light hurt his eyes and he hated her.

"Have you been drinking tonight, sir?"

Spatula's low growl erupted into a single, "WOOF."

"EASY." He showed the dog a threatening hand and Spatula, lit up now by flashlight, calmed and looked away.

He smiled up into the light. "Not tonight."

She turned her light on Spatula again. "How about him?"

He was quick. "Well, yeah, he's had a few but what can you do."

"He looks pretty bad." She did a good deadpan. He saw she was pretty, pretty in an intelligent way, and nothing mean about her except the uniform. They both watched Spatula sitting there with his tongue out and an eyebrow up, looking like one very stupid human.

"'S why I'm driving." He didn't smile either. He stared at her openly, feeling the twinkle in his eye and seeing his good looks register.

She stared back. Her magic emptied him and his breath caught in his throat. She let her smile rise. Then she chuckled like a buddy, looked to the next car and said easily, "Have a good night."

Her arm's automatic gesture aimed the flashlight beam ahead, illuminating the way for him. She was still smiling.

HE PULLED INTO THE GAS STATION DESPERATE FOR THE bathroom. Walking through the empty convenience store he felt eyed by the attendant, a small twerp with buzzcut and pimple scars. He hated using a bathroom when he wasn't buying gas. The twerp probably had to keep it clean and drunken bums coming in to use it while buying nothing naturally added to a guy's minimum-wage bad mood. Stuck under these loud flourescent lights, alone most of the night.

A sign on the locked door said, Obtain Key From Attendant.

"Pack of cigarellos, and I'd like the key, please." He put down a five which the guy pinched up on the fly.

He hadn't said the word in years. Cigarellos. It was a musical word. He hadn't smoked them since Patrice said they made him smell. He'd loved her that much. Years.

"The tipped? The plain?"

The twerp was standing there impatient with him for not supplying this detail.

"Tipped. And, what, maybe three, four packs of matches." Cigarellos often went out on you.

"Would you like three, or would you like four?" The little guy stood there, hand hovering insolently over a plastic fishbowl of match packs.

"I'd like three or four."

The voice made the guy look up at him and what he saw made him look quickly down. He brought the whole container of matches to the counter, a move half-insolent and half-nervous.

"Just take what you need."

He opened the till, made change, put seventy-odd cents on the counter and slid it to him.

"I gave you a ten."

"Well, no sir, it was a five."

"It was a ten."

"It was a five. See?" He lifted the five out of the tray as if that proved anything. He shook a bit holding the bill aloft, and he looked hard at the floor.

"It was a ten. So that five would be my change."

He put his hand out, not far, make the twerp come to him. He was aware of the tilt to his head, and of his eyes starting to sting, the result of not blinking, not blinking and never taking your eyes off a guy, aware that, free of Patrice he was free to do all this again, stuff that made her nervous and smoke that made him smell.

He wondered if a twerp with a buzzcut and earrings would call the cops over five bucks. He took the five dollar bill, slid it into his shirt pocket. He tucked the fishbowl of matches under his arm and walked it out to the car. Climbing in, he realized he'd forgotten all about peeing. What a thing adrenalin was. He couldn't go back in there now, it would be embarrassing.

THE BAR WAS CALLED MAGGIE'S AND AFTER USING THE facilities he was told by the young waitress that because of its location it was closing in five minutes and he couldn't order a whole jug, not if it was just him drinking it.

"What if I bring my dog in?"

She ignored him to study a wall poster, a gleaming white Porsche.

"Can I get a half-jug then?"

"You mean the mini?"

"Yeah. The mini."

"No."

He wrestled two pints out of her and downed the first in one go. Empty and smelling of new paint, Maggie's was the most depressing bar he'd experienced in some time. Besides him, over in a corner draining his last gin of the day was a retiree with a permanent, wet-lipped smile, dressed in powder-blue suit and white belt. Poor guy looked abandoned. Smiling always and at absolutely nothing, which made less sense than the permanent scowls you more often saw. Friendly face like that, you could tell he wasn't alone by choice. On a different night he would've joined the old guy and given him a teasing. Nor was there any point talking to the waitress, who appeared to be working on a premature permanent scowl. She looked hungry only to be away from here and anybody to do with the place, including him. Strange to be linked to a bar you've been in all of two minutes and hated yourself.

In the car he unwrapped the packaged hoagie and laid it on the floor. He started the engine and listened to the liquid and cellophane sounds of Spatula's fifteen-second meal. He started back up the hill, lighting a cigarello only when he could see the police cars.

He waited for her in a line of five or six cars, at his front bumper a white stretch limo. From cars going the other direction a Jeep had been plucked and parked, and you could see the poor sucker in the back of the cruiser, hunching under the dome light, blowing into a plastic straw.

Inhaling his first cigarello in years right on top of two fast pints was a mistake. It wasn't quite the whirlies but it was close, the kind of dizziness you normally fixed with a palm over an eye, which wasn't a pose to strike now. Hopefully it would pass in time. What a waste if he stayed dizzy — the idea was to get another look at her. Get another look and maybe, who knows. Really — who knows? It was the one question you could keep in your front pocket because no one, not even Patrice, ever had the answer to it.

That limo there, those smoked glass windows, you always wondered who it was, imagined someone rich and maybe famous having the fancy martini party, the big coke-fest, where in all likelihood it was just another stag goof-up, or a high school kid spending his summer-job money to give her the date-of-her-life and get himself laid. So who was in there? Smoked glass was arrogant and maddening. No matter who you pictured, they were having a better time than you. He edged closer and closer to the limo and gave it a nudge too soft for the driver to feel.

He could imagine Patrice in there, Patrice half-clothed, smiling sideways at some guy in that way which said she was onto you. Or giving you that look over the tops of her glasses, sitting upstairs in her beanbag chair, in her underwear, reading a book. Those glasses on her, what was it? How could the opposite of sexiness be sexy? It was the same reason he liked her only half-naked. Flesh caught in its little prison. Flesh behind bars. Cop here in her tough copsuit, the wild softness under, softness in a shell. She was leaning into the limo, laughing at some rich joke, seduced by the whole thing herself. She aimed her light at someone in the back, heard something, laughed again. They could legally drink back there, someone was offering her a cock-tail. Come to the party, some slickboy would be yelling. Michael Jordan's going to be there, and so is Elton John and Jimmy Hoffa. She was doing a little side-to-side dance step, listening. She was great the way she moved. You could almost see the shape of her legs inside the boxy man-pants. *Hey there, what are your thoughts on* cop-*ulation*?

His turn.

"Have you been drinking tonight, sir?" The same light in his face.

"Not like those guys." He brought his chin up indicating the limo pulling slowly away.

"*That*," she said, smiling beautifully, her teeth showing, "was a fiftieth wedding anniversary."

"No way."

"*Way*. It was *too* cute."

Jesus but he wanted to get her home and sit her back on the couch, let their lives come out.

"So you been out partying tonight sir?"

Cops and their formality.

"No, just my party animal here." He patted Spatula, which made the dog climb up to a sit and turn to him expectantly. "Keeps giving me the wrong address."

"Well maybe —"

The cop with the clipboard barked something and she pulled away to look. He turned himself and peered out the back window. In the distance a car had taken a fast U-turn.

She was waving him on with her light, waving all the cars on and trotting away. A cruiser revved, doors slammed, tires screeched.

His foot obediently off the brake, the car rolled forward. He kept watching her as she ran across the street and leaned into the other cruiser and started talking fast to another cop.

'Well maybe' what? Well maybe you should go straight home. *Well maybe* you should step out of the car. Her look — she'd given him a look. *Well maybe* I could give you an address where I'll be in an hour, waiting.

DAVY JONES WAS STILL FULL BUT PATRICE HAD LEFT. STEVE wasn't there either, not like him to leave early, and nor was Karl anywhere to be seen. He asked Ray at the bar if he'd noticed her leaving, and Ray wiped with his rag more carefully, pretending not to know.

He ordered a pitcher and lit a cigarello. Margaret, a waitress who hadn't liked him since he began calling her "Thatcher," came directly over to tell him that cigars weren't allowed.

"I used to smoke cigars in here all the time."

"Not any more."

"I thought cigars were, you know, sort of *chi chi.*"

"Not here they're not." Thatcher turned and left, probably not knowing what *chi chi* meant.

He kept his cigarello going, and lit another right after it, hoping to have another cigar conversation with somebody, but no one so much as looked at him. Those sitting closest were intently not looking at him.

He'd been staring, dizzy, at nothing, he didn't know how long, when he noticed the couple that had been in his gaze all along, a young pair, maybe twenty, and they had between them a monster-sized ice cream sundae thing, cherries and sauces and sparkles all over it, and lit sparklers stuck in the top, and they'd just ignited what must be brandy pooled at the bottom. She screamed and laughed at the flames just missing her face and hair. Jesus but where'd they get ice cream this time of night and how'd they get in here, what kind of magic? Thatcher and Ray hurried over to yell at them, but they couldn't help but smile and laugh themselves, a little sundae-fire was entertainment and wasn't going to kill anybody. People were clapping and yelling. The girl jumped up and ran to bend and kiss the guy deeply. You got the whole range in this bar, and at last call you could get more than that. You got movie stars in here, and millionaires duking it out. Lyle, the dental surgeon who'd once owned the place, would be in the back throwing up by now. Two years ago a dealer had killed another in the parking lot. And there were regulars, like him, who disappeared for a time but came back. And there were old friends who changed slowly, over the years wearing away to smaller versions of themselves.

There'd be no point hunting her down. If she was home she'd know it was him and she wouldn't come to the door or answer the phone. He went out to the pay phone anyway, realizing in advance how much this endless ringing would infuriate him, made worse by not knowing if she was home alone or home at all and no longer having the means, or the right, to find out even these basic facts. Or if her bare shoulders were pinned under the forearms of Steve, or Karl, or any one of the long-patient gents who drank here. All he knew was that there was no predicting who the new guy would be. Five years ago it had been *him*. And amazing, amazing — getting a sudden clear picture of himself and Patrice five years ago, he felt jealous enough to fight that man. This was pretty good, he'd have to remember it: jealous of his younger self and wanting to take him to the parking lot, punch himself out.

No longer dizzy but guts hot and churning, which is maybe what he'd sought all along in going to the phone, he returned to his table and made fast work of the half pitcher that was left.

IN THE TRUNK UNDER THE SLEEPING BAG HE FOUND THE six-pack he'd forgotten about. Bonus-beer always tasted best. It was Piper's, and he said to the leaping Orca on the label, his lips sticking way out like a Frenchman's, "Yooo loook beauteefool." He got in and started the car, letting Spatula lick his cheek almost to his mouth, Spatch always taking advantage of him when he was drunk. He ripped a can from its plastic ring, popped it and poured some in his hand, laughing silently that he'd never thought to give Spatch beer before. The old guy must be thirsty and a little couldn't hurt. Some was slopping on the seat. What the hell. The car would stink of beer but so what. He poured more into the folds of cellophane on the floor for Spatch to lap at his leisure.

Pounding out of the parking lot in reverse he was half-hoping to nudge someone's BMW but somehow his exit was clean. He shot along the waterfront's foggy mile then turned uphill, hitting the gas, hungry to get to her. He laughed to see how he'd been frowning rigidly to keep from swerving — he'd been sending that frown right down the lengths of his arms to keep them steady. This was fun. She'd still be working, or maybe they were stupid enough to pack up shop before the bars closed. Maybe they didn't do strategy, and like any job it all had to do with when their shift ended. *Hey,* he'd say, *hey I had to come back and ask you your name.* Say it soft so she'd have to lean in to hear. *Been thinking about you all night. I made a bet with myself you'd tell me when your shift ends.* Then he'd ask and she'd tell him her name. She wouldn't smile as she told him and it would be like getting right in there behind her badge, the skin softest with the badge over it. She would tell him her name and he would roll the dice, bring a beer up to the window-edge for her to lean in and sneak a sip, daring her with his eyes to see her job for what it is and how it shouldn't pin down who we are or what we do on a hot night after the bars get out and our shifts end.

The roadblock was still there at the top of the rise, more cruisers than ever now, she was there somewhere in the middle of it all, lights flashing, wild, an invitation to a fantastic party.

COMEDIAN TIRE

BUDDHISM SAYS THERE'S NO beginning nor end to suffering, so in that sense there's no beginning nor end to this story — which is also about how humour lives in the very heart of suffering, and pops up like a neon clown from its big black box.

The background to the story involves my brother Ron, who a year ago at age fifty had a stroke. He survived with huge holes in his memory, dragging a foot, slurring, and utterly pissed off. Apparently strokes at his age aren't so rare. But, though he's ten years older than I am, in the ugly stew of emotions his illness brewed for me, one of the worst was a sense of my own mortality. And then my guilt at that. Watching him limp around in terminal despair, how could I possibly think about myself? But he looks like me. At the root of myself I could trade places.

A month ago it got worse. Ron had a series of heavier strokes, was now truly demolished, dying — could die at any time from a next stroke — and was placed in extended care with elderly people who are similarly bedridden and waiting for death. Ron can no longer walk, talk, control his bowels, eat on his own. I can see he recognizes me, but my arrivals lift his spirits not one bit. Waiting for the final oblivion, he stares at game shows with the other, older residents, unable to ask someone to please turn off this pap and stick in a decent movie. Or whatever. I don't know if he could follow a movie, or if he wants one, but from his eyes I know that he hates what he's watching, the canned laughter blasting the room and its dying, demented, warehoused bodies.

With Ron in Vancouver, and me on the Island, my monthly planning involves working out when next I can steal two days to ferry over and visit. Kyle's soccer tournaments, our baby daughter Lily, my wife Leslie's work schedule, not to mention my own, plus dentists, doctors, barbecues. All fight my attempts to get over and see Ron, who I don't really want to see, and who maybe doesn't want to see me either. Add to this mix my car — an '89 minivan — which lately has been stalling at intersections. Leslie has demanded a tune-up for some time now, using the words "dangerous" and "Lily" in the same sentence. In my list of things to do, double underlined was the note, *Fix van, visit Ron*.

I'm within walking distance of one of those red and white retail establishments with the red garage bays, and I took it there for that reason. I'd heard general warnings about the place, but in other cities I'd gone there for basic servicing and nothing bad had come of it, aside from being dinged the expected unexpected extras. Lots of cars sat out front waiting to get in, a good sign. The van needed a tune-up is all, and anybody with dirty fingernails can do a tune-up. I asked the man behind the counter for an oil change and tune, and to call me if they found anything big. Maybe I could catch the ferry that night, visit Ron in the morning, then stop by his apartment and load up. That was part of the reason I was avoiding this next visit: Ron would not be going home again and his apartment needed cleaning out. He would no longer in life be needing his clothes, furniture, CDs. My parents were pressing me. Either I come pick up his stuff or they'd "just have to put it out in the street." I didn't want to go and sort through his stuff because then I would have to think about Ron. My connection to Ron.

Ron, you see, is a hard-assed guy. A racist right-winger. We've never agreed on much. We've used our age difference as an easy excuse not to talk. But to put Ron in a nutshell: when I was nine, and he was nineteen, Ron went to the States and enlisted to fight in Vietnam. (Over a thousand Canadians actually did that.) I vaguely recall him talking about "gooks," and remember thinking the whole idea pretty cool as I marched off with my crooked stick to shoot at shadows in the woods behind the house. Though he didn't see action he returned as gook-hating as ever, despite the peace movement in particular and the Age of Aquarius in general.

In the years we both lived at home, I never did get to know him well. I remember closed doors, lots of being ignored, a few bored shoves when I got too close. Years later, smirking, he bought me and my friends our first case of beer. In fairness I'll add that he was never unkind to my mother, and he had the sense to keep quiet about my father's summer in Kelowna. Ron and I communicated with severe, silent eye contact over that one, and I believe that's as intimate as we ever got.

It's been hard to admit to myself that I'm in no hurry to see him again, my own brother. The last time I visited Extended Care it was excruciating to watch him being lifted out of bed for his bath. His eyes were sunken and he'd lost his muscle. They use this wheeled crane that hoists a body up in a canvas sling. An attendant on each arm. Slowly airborne, Ron began to panic, or maybe it was pain — eyes bugging, he whimpered and slobbered and both hands clawed and convulsed minutely. He looked pleadingly to me and all I could do was avoid his eyes and smile a smile so hollow it said that all was fine because now he was going to have his nice bath. Half the horror came out of questions coming at me over the hum of the crane motor: How do I feel for this man who is my brother? What is carried in genes and what does the word "brother" mean? Here is a man I'd avoid if I weren't related to him. He is suffering in ways I can't comprehend and might be better off dead. Do I want him dead? For what reasons, exactly?

THE GARAGE PLACE CALLED ME LATE THAT AFTERNOON, saying they'd indeed found serious problems. As a matter of course they'd conducted their "21-point inspection" and found the van lacked rear brakes, the emergency cable was frozen, and the horn didn't work. The total cost would be $700.

"The stalling," I said. "Did you find the reason for the stalling?" The brakes had been feeling okay to me, and I'd known about the emergency cable, rusted in place by New Brunswick road salt some six years ago. I guess I never used the horn.

"It's stalling?"

"I brought it in because it's stalling. When you stop at a light it idles really — "

"That's your basic tune-up," he said.

"Okay. I just want the tune-up. And an oil change please."

"I really, really wouldn't advise you driving it off the lot with no rear brakes." He paused, during which time I closed my eyes. "I couldn't help noticing your baby seat? It's not my business to say, but — "

"Okay. Forget the horn, forget the emergency cable. Go ahead on the rear brakes."

"Go ahead then?"

"Yes."

He said it would be ready by noon.

THAT NIGHT I WAS TELLING LESLIE HOW ODD IT WAS, RON'S present situation. At his age so feeble, and him a man who'd always valued, and assumed, his physical strength. He'd worked mainly in heavy equipment (pretending he was driving a tank, I joked to myself), for the last decade building local wharves with a pile-driving outfit. He often had his shirt off, and grease on his considerable chest muscles. He was one of those guys you see yelling to other guys over the roar of machinery, their shoulders glowing bigger than their hardhats.

But what I was describing to Leslie was that virtually all the attendants in extended care were Asian. Here was a man who'd never seen fit to distinguish between Chinese, Japanese, Vietnamese, whomever. They were small, sly, and in his country for no good reason. I'd not heard the word for a while: gooks. And now, bedridden, unable to move or speak, Ron was being tended to by gooks.

I described the scene to Leslie. Ron, already pissed off at his traitorous body, and here's this stream of Asian caregivers — most were Philippino actually — dressing him, sponging his private parts, feeding him his baby food, and keeping up a gay, accented banter: *Okay, Ron! How you do today! Boy, you big! You getting bigger I think!* Talking to him like a child as they stripped or sponged or fed. I found I couldn't begrudge them their lack of sincerity. A job like that, it was amazing that they managed to feign cheer.

But the look in Ron's eyes. As if he were assessing a persistent and violently bad dream. I tried to describe it to Leslie. She used the word "karma." I pictured one of Dante's poetic hells.

Ron's situation — his being tended by cheerful, fast-moving Asians — is something I would have liked to ask him about. I tell myself there's lots about Ron I would like to learn, but I wonder if that's because now it's impossible. Another thing I've wanted to ask: did he know what he was doing when he was pretending to shoot gooks? He would fire his air machine gun and make a sound that was exactly "Buddha-Buddha-Buddha-Buddha."

AT NOON THE NEXT DAY MY VAN SAT OUT ON THE LOT, READY. I entered and announced myself. A long and detailed receipt chugged its way out of the computer. A fellow with "Kyle" on his chest, but no grease under his nails, cheerfully told me I owed $950.

Leslie says I don't stand up for myself. It's true: while not exactly a wimp, I do turn the other cheek. Without going into too much detail here — it's the kind of garage-hell everyone has experienced, after all — I'll just say I did myself proud. First I calmly stated the obvious logic, that since I'd told them to do *less* work than the $700 quote would have paid for, the amount I now owed could not possibly be *more*. Kyle cheerfully said he'd add up the figures again, and did.

"Nope, it's $950," Kyle chirped. He showed me, jabbing his finger on the receipt, how they'd replaced my emergency cable, done my brakes, the horn, lots of labour involved. At the head of the list was the 21-point inspection, for which I was being charged a cute $21.

"I told the guy on the phone to change the oil, tune it and do the rear brakes. That's it. Not the other stuff."

"Well, no sir, you were talking to me, and you said, 'Go ahead.'"

"No I — Well, yeah, go ahead on *the rear brakes*." I jabbed my own finger onto the sheet. "I'm *not* paying for that inspection because I didn't even *want* an inspection, I wanted a *tune-up*." By now a trap door in my gut was swinging open, and I was well into that icy sweat of futility.

"Not what I heard, sir. You said —"

"Even if you *did* all that stuff, it still can't be more than $700. That was the quote. It can't *possibly* be —"

"It was an estimate, sir."

And so on. In the end I loudly threatened (a first for me) to tell my friends about this; I had a lot of friends (a lie) and they all drove shitty cars like mine and used places like this frequently but would no longer. I almost said that I was a writer and that *I'll write about this place*. I did say I would pay no more than the quoted $700. I would drive my van away (though my key hung from a hook on his wall behind the counter) and they could call the police if they wished. In fact, *please do*.

Two other customers watched me, perhaps entertained. Kyle wore a practiced poker face, not a tiny muscle of which had yet twitched. We stared at each other. I sensed victory. He said he'd "go through the numbers and see what he could do." After five minutes of crossing out and typing, and a new bill chugging out, he told me he'd been able to get it down to $750. I stomped out clutching my key, feeling utterly defeated in victory, having paid

$750 for a tune-up. Well, I had new rear brakes and an emergency cable I might one day use. Maybe I'd honk at someone.

My van was surrounded by other cars, shining in the sun. The garage bays were empty. It struck me that all these parking-lot cars were decoys, brightly-painted mallards floating on this cement suburban pond, luring in foolish ducks like myself. Driving the two blocks home, I felt I was riding in a fragile creature, a victim of unwanted transplants.

THAT EVENING I PHONED MY PARENTS, WHO HAD WORRIED when I hadn't shown up. Again they murmured disapproval of my "letting all Ron's things go to waste," though there were still two days before the end of the month when his apartment had to be cleared out. It struck me how the elderly hate chaos, what they call "leaving things to the last minute." Maybe the notion of "the last minute" takes on fatal implications. I didn't explain my hesitations about weeding through Ron's private stuff. Since his second wife left he'd been living alone for almost ten years. I didn't tell them that poking through my brother's things would feel like climbing right up into his angry armpit. I said I'd leave tomorrow morning and be there in the afternoon.

"Good," said my mother. "Ron really wants to see you."

IN THE MORNING WHEN I STARTED THE VAN, STEPPED ON the brake and put it in reverse to commence backing out, the brake pedal went *smish*, right to the floor. I *smished* it a few times in disbelief. I turned it off, got out, saw the thin stream of brake fluid running the length of the driveway to the reddish pool on the street.

This was good, this was comedy — $750 to have my brakes *broken*. What if I'd driven right out into traffic? I stomped inside, swearing and laughing. Leslie shook her head yelling, "You're kidding!" and little Lily started to cry. I phoned the garage. It wasn't Kyle, but in about twenty words I got my message across and the fellow, blandly apologetic, said a tow truck would be there soon. Lily was loud now and I could hardly hear myself demanding that the van be driven back to my house when it was fixed, and I wanted this done by lunch because I had a ferry to catch. I was all-business, macho, a new me. I'd never considered Ron a role model, and didn't now. Him looming up behind me, a smirking spectre, likely had to do with how much he'd occupied my thoughts lately. What would Ron have done? Well, he wouldn't have taken it *there* in the first place. And he wouldn't have given them a *fucking dime*. In fact, he would've just tuned 'er up himself.

TWO THAT AFTERNOON I CALLED THE GARAGE ASKING where my car was. (I had to restrain Leslie from taking the phone and yelling at someone. She can do that sort of thing with ease.) The man checked and said it was just coming into the bay. I said I was promised noon, I said I needed to catch a ferry. I almost said something about needing to go see a dying brother.

The van was delivered at five. The driver, a kid, and oblivious to the history of injustice, was no one to yell at. He seemed to expect thanks for this special service so I thanked him. He said, "Your right drum coupling wasn't on right, so out she came." He looked at me as if I should have known that.

I phoned my parents, tried to explain but ended up apologizing. Tomorrow, I promised. My mother got in that Ron had really wanted to see me today.

IN THE MORNING I REPACKED MY DAY-BAG AND WAS THROWING some rope into the van (I figured to bring back a chair or dresser of Ron's, if only for show) when Leslie hurried out with Lily in her arms. Lily had thrown up, had a high fever, and Leslie had arranged a quick visit with the doctor. She'd be back in an hour. I nodded and kissed Lily's hot little head. Leslie smiled sadly for me, knowing well my dealings with Ron and my parents, having heard about it so much. She looked big-eyed and feverish herself.

I went back inside to make myself breakfast. The phone rang as I was flipping eggs. It was my mother. Her voice sounded oddly full of strength.

"He's had another. We're at his hospital. They think this is it this time. It's affecting the swallowing and the breathing."

"Is it — I should — "

"You should be here right now."

I said I was on my way, and I hung up. Staring at the clock, my heart beating, I calculated doctors' waiting rooms, traffic, ferries. Behind these calculations, something was weighing my desire: did I want see Ron die, or did I want to miss it?

But the comedy that had begun a few days ago was accelerating. Like *deus ex machina,* the phone rang again. It was Leslie and she was hysterical.

"*We almost — The car — almost killed us — These bastards —*"

"What's wrong? How's Lily? What happened?"

"It was hardly running, and I was passing, right by so I turned in — It stalled — A truck had to screech to — We almost — "

I got from her that they were at the red garage. I ran the five blocks. The van was parked haphazardly, at a diagonal, blocking two garage bays, the driver's door still open. I was huffing and dizzy as I pushed in the door. What I walked into instantly cleared my head.

My wife held Lily, who was red and mouth-breathing. Confronting the young man behind the counter, my wife was red too and breathing heavily herself. She had been yelling. The young man, a comedian wearing the overalls of someone named "Lisa," was smiling defensively.

"No, no. I worked on that van," he told her. "You're saying you want a tune-up?"

Spontaneously, my wife vomited. Angrily, her eyes on him. I don't know if her joining the comedy was deliberate. It's the kind of thing Leslie could probably do if she wished. But here in the aftermath stood "Lisa," and Leslie, and Lily, and me.

I think we'd all stopped breathing. In that second before anyone could move, the world was clarified.

Everyone has known a place that, for a moment, stands vastly, maybe religiously, crystal. Mine, my alter, was a garage waiting room. I could feel the blood-pounding squeeze of shoes on my feet. Could register the three-headed candy machine with its glass offerings of cashews, sour fruits and jelly beans. I understood that my van's engine had been built in Asia. Could feel my complex hurry to see my dying brother, but would never know if he was worth hurrying to. Or if he had a sense of humour for bodies and cars breaking down, for the junk that lives do become. Here was feverish little Lily, my feelings for whom were untamed and sacred. Here was my wife, who likely had the flu herself but was possibly enjoying herself in ways I couldn't know. Here was this guy, "Lisa," who lacked training in what had just happened, and in what was happening now.

That is, clarity with no meaning to it at all. Lisa in control. This red garage.

THE LITTLE DRUG ADDICT THAT COULD

*J*ACK STARED AT THE SCREEN, UNABLE to focus, a Friday afternoon. An eyebrow ticked somewhat in time to a finger pecking the keyboard. He was recording more bad news, except for a few coho runs in Juan de Fuca that looked solid. The Commercials were already lobbying for them, as were the Sporties, who claimed the tourism industry would break down if they were denied access to these particular salmon. Jack kept shaking his head. He was in a hurry to leave the office but had forgotten why, until he remembered: Tyson. His nephew was coming today.

Fine, screw it. He stashed some files in his briefcase, tucked his laptop under his arm and wished Jasmine and Nancy a good weekend, giving Nancy the nudge-wink because of her rumoured new boyfriend — she had thick glasses and had been long alone, and inclusion in any office naughtiness thrilled her. Jack left down the back stairs, avoiding Parker and the rest.

In his new Astro van he belted up and punched number five on the CD player, "Dazed and Confused." He'd felt squirrelly and squeezed all day, time to let loose. He upped the volume and cracked the window, not minding that street kids might look up to see an old guy nodding his head to old Zeppelin. He buzzed open the moon-roof, too — why not turn the van into a big speaker? This vehicle was the first toy he'd bought himself in years and years.

Tyson had called that morning to ask if he could visit and, more mysteriously, stay awhile, asked if Jack still lived in "that same place with the basement space." It felt odd being called "Uncle Jack." Tyson was, what, thirty-two? Jack being fifteen years older. Which was about how long since they'd seen each other, and this with Tyson living just across the water in Vancouver. Jack heard lots from his sister, though. Anne would say, "Ty's between jobs," or, "He still hasn't found his niche," but, as with the fish farm job he'd arranged for Tyson up on Redonda, Jack knew his nephew was in the habit of being fired. He remembered the foreman at Redonda phoning to say, "Bastard sleepin' in or not even showin' up. Just wanna let ya know your nephew's got problems, eh?" Jack had told the foreman to do what he had to do.

Nephew — one of the weirder words in the language.

JACK FINISHED HIS THIRD BEER WATCHING TYSON CLIMB out of the taxi. As if surprised by the rain on his head, Tyson looked up at the heavy clouds. The driver popped the trunk and lifted out Tyson's little Nike bag. That was it for luggage. The bag was tiny in the cabby's hand but big in Tyson's, and Jack appreciated again how bird-frail his nephew was. Not freakishly small but oddly so because Tyson's parents were sizable. Jack recalled his sister's guilty moanings about her smoking through her pregnancy. To this day she'd go into a deep stare whenever talk of smoking and childbirth came up. The boy's failures she probably felt to be hers and, seeing that, Jack was fine with the fact that he'd never had kids.

Tyson paid the cabby and gazed up at the house. Jack stepped back from the window.

He'd tidied up a bit, realizing as he put away the popcorn maker, hung frypans, and stacked empty beer cases out on the deck, how rarely he had company these days. These years. Hadn't "entertained" much, as Diane would have put it. Cleaning up, he'd thought about Diane, understood it had been six years since the divorce. Time flies when you're having ... He noted his chair positioned three feet from the TV. Diane never would have allowed it. He turned the chair back into the "conversation circle" but the four leg-dents in the carpet at the TV looked permanent. The chair's armrests were grey with scrubbed spillage, its cushions concave with his evenings of news, nature shows and hockey.

THEY SAT AT THE KITCHEN TABLE. JACK HAD PUT ON *LIFE'S Rich Pageant*, his one REM disc, in deference to his nephew's age. Tyson didn't acknowledge the music; he still had his wet coat on. Those bedroom eyes, lazy yet piercing, princely; the dark thick eyebrows that almost met. He was skinnier than Jack remembered him to be, and it looked like he hadn't slept. But he was calm.

"I'm asking you a big favour, Uncle Jack."

"Ah — sure." Jack did a comic grimace. "Wait. How big?"

"Big." Tyson didn't smile. "Big. First, please just promise you won't tell Mom."

Money. Thirty-two-year-old fuckup doesn't want mommy to know he's a leech as well as a failure.

"Okay. But only if it isn't about her. Something that'll affect —"

"Not about her at all. It'll hurt her only if she knows."

"Do you need some money?"

Tyson snorted and smiled. "Well, yeah! Why not? But that's not it, no. More serious than that."

Jack nodded. Tyson didn't look upset about something. He seemed ironic and unconcerned, serious only in the stagy sense of trying to sound it, and mostly to himself.

"Okay. Tell me the deal. *Mano a mano.*" Jack had never said this before and enjoyed saying it.

"Well, Uncle Jack, I'm addicted to heroin, and I want to use your place to kick."

DOWNSTAIRS, JACK SHOWED HIM THE BEDROOM OFF THE rec room that was never used either. They opened windows for air. Jack went up for blankets and pillows, Tyson calling after him, "Where are the wall manacles, I need wall manacles."

Jack tore through the bedding closet looking for stuff, his heart going pretty good. He saw he wasn't upset but excited. Jesus — entertained. Well, you didn't get this every day. Too bad for Anne, sure, but Tyson was right, it had nothing to do with her. Jack saw his hand was going back and forth from the good burgundy sheets to the old whites. Which? What exactly would happen down there? Jack lifted out the burgundy sheets. Tyson was a guest, and what they were dealing with here was maybe just a lot of sweating. The white sheets looked a bit hospital. On his way down he detoured through the kitchen for a couple of beers.

He was aware of acting cool, casual, with his nephew. Cold turkey, sure thing, no sweat, do it all the time myself, we're all junkies here. He recalled this same urge to fake familiarity from being a teenager, when a bit of danger came along, as in a bar when someone slid by offering "Acid?" and heart pounding you'd shrug, nonchalantly toss off that "Nah."

"You grab that side."

He handed Tyson a corner of fitted sheet. They had the width confused with the length, and halfway into their second try Jack started giggling. Tyson raised his eyebrows.

"A bureaucrat and a junkie," Jack explained, "trying to make a bed."

Tyson smiled briefly.

"Hey," Jack added. "I'm not judging."

"Judge away. I judge bureaucrats all the time."

They finished the bedding, and while Tyson stashed his belongings in the little dresser, Jack fiddled with the curtains. This room must be safe from neighbours' eyes. They sat on the bed and each opened a beer. Tyson sipped once without thirst.

"Okay, so." Jack had waited before initiating this next step. "What do you want from me? Want me to leave you alone?"

"I got a plan," Tyson said.

He stood and opened the top dresser drawer, drawing from it a shaving kit that he brought back to the bed, unzipping it as he moved. With efficient respect he lifted out and lined up on the bed two black film canisters, blackened spoon, candle, syringe, cotton balls. The syringe was thin as a pencil, contemporary. Jack thought, "Euro."

"This" — Tyson lifted one canister — "is what I have left. It'll get me through until I go to sleep, probably sometime tonight." Tyson met Jack's eye. "I haven't slept in a while just so I could sleep tonight. Been planning this, right?"

Jack nodded and Tyson lifted and rattled the other cannister.

"Two major fat sleeping pills for tonight, they'll let me sleep way into tomorrow, get me through some of the early shit. God" — Tyson shook his head and blinked — "if I could sleep five days it'd be a snap." He shook the canister again. "And then, sixteen forty-mill valium to keep things down a bit. And can I move that TV in here?" Tyson tilted his head toward the rec room.

"No cable. You like CBC?"

"Maybe I could rent a VCR? You mind that?"

"No, no, sure. Hey just take mine. I'll bring it down."

"Great." Tyson sat nodding, staring straight ahead. For the first time, he looked serious. "Great," he repeated, more softly.

"Sounds like a plan, then."

The two men sat quietly for a moment. Jack had plenty of questions but could see that Tyson was absorbed in this task he'd set himself and that no one else had a role to play. It was unnerving, though, sitting here with this little man. Because somehow, here on the bed, this nephew, this junkie loser sister's-boy, radiated a perverse status, and he even seemed to know it, but didn't care, making the status all the more weighty; it was the power of celebrity, of what it was to be society's supreme bogeyman, to inhabit a world poor straight Uncle Jack knew nothing about.

"I'm going to have to fix soon. Should I use the bathroom?"

"Whatever. I don't care." We're all just junkies here.

Tyson took a pack of matches from his shirt pocket and dropped it into the equation. He was visibly more restless. "Soon" meant "now." And it had come on out of nowhere.

"So — why here, Tyson? We hardly know each other. How'd you know I wouldn't just, I don't know, 'freak out.' Call the cops."

Tyson smiled and looked up at Jack, while his fingers, using eyes of their own, got busy with his things.

"Cops are the least of my worries, man. I mean, jail would be one way to do this." He took his beer from between his thighs and raised it in ironic toast. "No beer in jail, though. No Valium. No movies. No dozen James Bonds back-to-back. I think James Bond and *Star Wars* might do the trick. Action."

"Why not, you know, friends? Why me?" Jack half-expected, or perhaps half-hoped, to hear something about family.

"Because you're bigger than me. You can wrestle me down." A joke. Everybody was bigger than him. "I don't know, Uncle Jack." Tyson furrowed his brow but his answer remained well-crafted. "I guess I don't really have friends any more who aren't users. And you wouldn't call them friends. Which is one reason I'm doing this."

Jack didn't know what "doing this" referred to — quitting or injecting. Tyson was drawing a length of rubber tube from his shaving kit.

When Tyson fit the candle in its holder, placed it on the dresser and lit it, Jack stood, waggling his empty bottle.

"How's your beer?"

"I'm fine." Tyson glanced at the full beer on the floor beside his foot.

Jack left to fetch one for himself, disappointed Tyson hadn't understood he was being funny. He decided to hang out upstairs until his nephew wandered up.

JACK ATE HIS MICROWAVED BURRITOS SITTING AT THE kitchen table, feeling odd for it. He always ate at this time in front of the television and was aware of missing the evening news and some stories he'd been following. For some reason he hadn't wanted Tyson to catch him eating at the TV, so he sat with his laptop opened in front of his plate, its screen showing a complex of pink and green bars. A cute colour choice, the pink represented past sockeye counts at various Sitka River streams. The green bars, far shorter than the pink, represented this year's returning salmon.

Tyson came up and sat with him. He was calm again. Jack stole little glances. Tyson looked normal enough. Though his eyes didn't seem to care what they were looking at. He sat straighter now, but it was as if his shoulders were held up by invisible hooks. Jack didn't bother offering him any dinner. You could just tell.

With his fork, tapping until Tyson looked, Jack indicated an empty bar that lacked any green at all.

"They logged too close here and — see? Nothing. Spawners all sat there at the mouth, this big logjam blocking it. Just hung around till they died. That run is now extinct. Not a big one, but still."

"So what's this unit worth?" Tyson nodded minutely in the direction of the computer.

"I dunno, the office bought it. Four, maybe five." Jack almost laughed saying this. Telling a junkie what his laptop was worth. Hey Tyson, here's the keys to the new van, why dontcha take her for a spin?

"They won't go to another stream?" His nephew's eyes had focused on the screen.

"They won't. Can't."

"How do they even know?"

"We figure it's two things. Out at sea, it's some sort of magnetic sense keeps them in touch with the poles, with basic direction. Once they're close, inshore, we figure it's smell. They smell something that's different in their stream from the one just a half mile away."

Tyson sat staring too intently at the graph. "They're on rails, man."

"That's right," Jack agreed, though his nephew seemed to be referring to the graph itself, which did look like rails, rather than to the genetic imperative of salmon.

"Anyway, yeah, Mom told me once you used to be into it a bit."

It took Jack a moment to see that, apropos of nothing, Tyson was now answering his earlier question.

"You mean, what, dope?"

"I mean, in general. Yeah."

Jack shrugged, aware as he did so how pathetic it was to be letting Tyson read this as an affirmative. What had Anne said about him? It was Anne who had been the more experimental by far, her crowd taking to psychedelics and the whole bit. No sense telling Tyson that. It was decades ago. Jack's own claim to druggy fame was the time he'd tried what was ostensibly mescaline but nothing happened. No sense telling Tyson that either. Otherwise, there had been the ubiquitous pot at weekend parties. Jack had been stoned plenty but couldn't recall ever buying any.

"My reputation's unearned."

"Yeah, well. I knew at least you'd be sympathetic or something."

"But you really think I might have to, what, pin you down?"

Chewing, Jack smiled and shook his head for him. "I mean, if things get weird are you expecting me to — what?"

"*No,* no." Tyson shrugged his little shoulders. "I just needed a place. And it would be a bit harder, here, to get some." He looked up and found Jack's eye. "To get more. When 'things get weird.'"

"So how weird will things get?"

From the way Tyson spoke, Jack could tell he'd said it before.

"It'll be like this: twenty years of heaven will flip upside down and squeeze into one week of hell."

"It's not your first time trying this, sounds like."

Tyson nodded. "No sense pinning me down. If I want it, I'll get it. I just needed a place." He gave Jack what was meant to be a profound look. "I'm not that bad."

"Well, no, Tyson, I know you're not."

Tyson laughed. "I mean my using. I'm not that bad. It's been worse than this. Most guys are *way* worse than this. But it's been getting pretty bad so it was time. Sort of a now-or-never thing."

"You can do it."

Tyson nodded, staring at the table. He moved his arms in feeble, cycling punches. "I think I can. Chuga-chuga."

"So what's it like? I have to ask. Heroin."

Tyson sighed. He sat back, professorial. "'Heroin. What's it like'. Well. One guy, dead now — man, years go, dead years ago — said it pretty good. Said it was like nursing."

"Nursing."

"As in sucking the big, beautiful breast. Not just any breast. *Mother's* breast. The *best* mother's breast. It's like" — Tyson brightened with a new addition to his dead friend's words —

"it's like sucking *Eve's* breast."

Jack pictured Anne, pictured her thirty years ago. He thought he could recall her nursing this man right here.

Tyson was still adding to it. "And it's also, at the same time, *sex* with her."

"Tyson, you can do it."

"I can." Tyson sat nodding, staring deeply again. Perhaps it had been a mistake getting him to think of why he liked heroin in the first place.

"Just gotta" — Jack reddened, listening to himself — "just gotta, you know, stay positive."

"You're right." Tyson stopped nodding. "You know, it's not even that addictive. No, I mean it *is* addictive." Tyson snorted, jabbed a giant phantom needle in his arm. "I mean, 'hey,' right? But, at the start, no. It takes a while. You almost have to want to be."

"I've heard that."

"Have to want — Eve. Sex with Eve. *Sleepy* sex with Eve."

"And now it's time" — Jack felt clever saying this — "for the divorce."

"Stay positive, week of hell, then off I go."

"Then off you go ... Where to, Tyson? When the week's done. You have plans?"

"It's one thing at a time, man. Gotta do this thing first, and then — "

"Sorry, sorry, you're right. Keep your mind on the matter at —"

"No, no, plans are good, plans are good. Gotta have something to do, right?"

"You do."

"Well I have this sort of new job — the job I have now you don't wanna know about." Tyson's smile was engagingly criminal. "This new one's selling boats. Friend's father is a yacht broker? Used yachts. Huge, major boats. Some from Asians going back to Hong Kong, some from drug runners gone down. Big, nice boats. One has an indoor pool."

"Holy."

"Just one of those little things where you swim against a current in one spot, but you get to say, 'And this one has an indoor pool.'" Tyson gestured elegantly over Jack's burritos to an invisible yacht, laughed, then brought his hand back to press under his nose as he sniffed violently, and coughed.

Jack had to look away. Picturing Tyson sniffing on the job, he smiled as he asked, "Commission work?"

"Yup. Keeps ya hoppin. Gotta smile a lot." He sniffed again.

"Don't smile too much."

"Boats like that sell themselves," Tyson offered, dismissive, and Jack was made to consider that his nephew might be right, and even that he might do well selling yachts.

"Know why this father-guy hired me?"

"No."

"Because I'm small. He told me he liked his 'people in sales' to be small, because when they walked around on a boat they made the boat look bigger."

Jack took his nephew in at a glance, feeling sorry for him, Tyson's eyes — now glassy and red-rimmed — the only big thing about him. One of Disney's baby bugs. Jack supposed that if you were small your whole life you did get used to it.

And small people could own a spark, verging on anger, that delivered them from failure.

"Tyson, you want to, I don't know, 'do' anything tonight?" He felt foolish saying this; his nephew was staring at him he could have been a chair. At the same time he understood that you could say anything to a junkie. "I have no internal organs" — he would have received the same look.

Jack added, "Though I guess you're already 'doing' it, aren't you?"

Tyson, present after all, smiled for him and nodded.

Checking his nephew's beer — still his first, halfway down, flat as apple juice — Jack went to the fridge for one of his own.

"So Tyson — maybe I'll be your first customer. I need a boat."

"Great." Not at all believing.

"I can afford a dinghy off the ass-end."

Tyson's mouth and eyebrows worked together and almost managed a true smile. "I guess you're still into the fishing and all that?"

"Yeah. Well, not so much lately. Which is one reason for a boat. So no, really, I do want a decent boat someday. Soon."

Jack sat down with his beer, clicking shut the laptop screen as he did. He felt voluble with all the beer, he'd had five or six now, why not, it was a Friday night, and not a typical one either. Who knew what would happen?

"Visit me and we'll do a deal." Tyson spoke with the poker face of a professional, and it was unclear whether he was serious, or mocking Jack, or mocking the profession altogether.

"Maybe we will."

Jack was serious. The notion, long buried, had sprouted through simply saying it. Up until ten years ago he'd always had something, usually a small runabout, something he could trailer most weekends to this inlet or that, combining pleasure and work. He'd fished famously all through his twenties and thirties. He'd cut back due to pressures at work, and cut back completely when he sensed, too late, that more time spent with Diane might save them.

"You guys deal in any around the twenty-eight, thirty-foot range?"

"I think I saw some that size." Tyson absently cleaned his fingernails. "Sure, yeah," he offered suddenly. "I wouldn't mind maybe hitting a bar or something. Watch some women walk by."

"Okay." Jack stepped to the fridge and twisted the top off a fresh beer. "But I'm serious. I'm going to go fishing again. I'm coming over to see you and buy a boat."

Jack felt that good twinge of having a fishing trip in the morning, a little grip in the gut that focused in hope the variables of weather, tides, feed in the area, the bite.

"Hey." Tyson stretched luxuriously. "I'll be there."

Jack knew in this same gut that his favourite times had been on the water, river mouths especially. Drifting, he'd stand and strip-cast buzz bombs into the passing pools, hot from the sun but cool underfoot, the water emerald and lens-like, so the big-eyed, hunting salmon appeared bigger than they really were.

Jack got to his feet, hoisting his beer in the air. "Hey — I mean I've *got* to. I'm *dying* here."

"Well," said Tyson, "change your scene then."

A thirty-footer, even a twenty-six — he could live on. He would tow a cartop for forays upriver. Tie up to the mother ship in the evening. Quit his job. Sell the house. He could do contract work, fish counting. Maybe some guiding. He would eat fish. There'd be one of those small barbecues bolted to the stern deck railing. There'd be a small TV, or not. He could get by. It was impossible, but he could.

"Gotta get out of this *hole* I'm in, Tyson. I mean it."

"Hey. Do it."

"You know" — Jack was pacing now — "my van down there? Bought it a month ago. You know that *new smell* in it is the most satisfying thing in my life that's happened in *years*?"

Looking edgier, Tyson glanced up at his uncle and back to the table again.

"I mean" — Jack leaned at his nephew, his eyes wide — "a *smell*?"

"Not good."

Jack paced, did some quick math. "You know I haven't had sex for over *a thousand days*?" You can say anything to a junkie.

"That's a long time," offered his nephew, who appeared not to know, or care, if his uncle was complaining or bragging.

"You know what? You're quitting heroin? Well, hey: I'm quitting my life."

"Sounds good."

"I'm not that drunk."

"I know."

"Tyson, I'm serious. I'm going to buy a boat from you."

"Let's do it."

SO THIS WAS EVE'S BREAST.

They sat on stools at the bar at the Crown and Thorn, watching women walk by. One waitress — feline yet friendly, skin a tawny cream — was worth watching. Jack pointed out how her left, tray-bearing shoulder was bigger than her right, but Tyson stared at soccer highlights on the TV. He grunted as a wiry black player on the mostly white German team performed an upside-down bicycle kick to drive the ball off the crossbar.

"More for me then," Tyson murmured.

Jack had just turned down Tyson's offer of a second injection. A "chip," Tyson had called getting it in the shoulder. An hour ago, in the men's washroom, the two of them crammed in one cubicle, Tyson squatting on the seat, Jack had received his chip. His turning down a second had nothing to do with anything, other than the first one was fine, still fine. A second didn't matter.

Jack stared at his Guinness, nodding in a logical, affirmative rhythm to its thousands of bubbles moving. Heroin did a wise thing with time; it harmonized all of time's possibilities because there was no competition between any of them. Jack hadn't spoken for maybe ten minutes, but he knew he could add to what he'd said then, which was that he found "nursing on Eve" to be a fine summing up.

"But it's less hungry than that. I mean" — Jack waited for Tyson to look from the TV to him — "are you hungry, at all?"

Tyson smiled, turned back to the soccer.

"It does everything, even the sucking. It's more like being in the breast itself."

Tyson nodded once, bored by a neophyte's persistence.

"But I can't really see staying in it. Staying here."

"No," Tyson agreed softly.

"We can grow up."

"We can." Tyson watched the patterned flow of bodies, and added, "But, ooo, it's a warm bath, isn't it?"

Jack didn't want to fall to the simple truth of this. He flexed his shoulders in a slow roll, feeling the vestiges, sweet and sour now, of muscular ecstasy. Not even ecstasy mattered. Nor did its loss. Nor did a thousand days, or the impossibility of that feline waitress. There were no edges here. Jack knew he could smash his head down through his glass of Guinness, slicing his face and busting his nose on the oak bar-top — and it wouldn't be all that interesting. Thoughts, objects — this oak grain, this waitress' fingers, his feeling for them — revealed a gleam that was utterly true, and yet did not inspire.

Maybe he'd been a bit drunk, but he regretted nothing. It had been a simple evening. Jack had decided to quit his life, Tyson had decided to buy more heroin. They'd driven downtown, Jack had had a few so Tyson drove. He parked and disappeared into one dingy apartment building, then another, while Jack nursed a beer in the passenger seat, the van idling, Enya on low. They'd come here. Here they were. He'd met and sucked sweet Eve, but it didn't matter. What mattered was that he'd made a decision.

"You can have my van."

"What?"

"I'll sign my van over to you tonight, if you want it. But it has to be tonight."

"Sure." Tyson turned his head Jack's way but his eyes stayed on the screen. "Why."

Jack couldn't voice his thoughts, for they weren't quite thoughts, having more to do with this oak grain, with seeing its pace of aging, solidifying, greying, dying, even under the hard varnish. In fifty years it would look different, though its only movement would have been a kind of gathering, which he could feel now, in his abdomen.

"It's a sort of symbol."

"Cool."

"You're probably not going to quit tonight, right?"

"Probably not."

"I am."

With the onset of a commercial, Tyson turned to him confidently. His tiny body was perfect for the time being, his smile a platter of insincerity, his eyes lords of knowing.

"You can do it."

THE HANGOVER

KEITH HADN'T WANTED TO DO this camping trip with his brothers at all. Here he was, sitting rigid in this iffy tin boat zipping across Georgia Strait, only because he feared what they would have done had he not shown up. It would have taken the form of a prank, Phil and Raymond giggling into his dream, looming out of the darkness by his bedside at some ungodly hour, as when they were kids — though grotesque now for their grey hair and paunches. They would have dragged him out and made him drink scotch. As when they were kids: all fun, but not. Let's get our stuffy cellist brother drunk. When Phil called last month to suggest the trip, he announced himself with, "Is this the cello guy?"

Their little boat was so low in the water Keith could wet his fingers without leaning over. One freak wave — no, the term was 'rogue' — one rogue wave was all it would take. How long could you survive in this water, life jacket or not? His brothers would not even have begun to consider this, a subject for worry-warts; a subject, they'd imply with amused glances at each other, for Keith. Macho, they were sitting on their life vests, using them as cushions. Keith was aware how childlike he must look in his, the proud puffy orange chest riding so high he could rest his chin on it — which was rather nice actually. It wasn't often you could release your neck. And it was a warm comfort to tuck his hands in behind the life vest too. He knew his brothers had taken note and traded looks. But he loved keeping his hands tucked away, safe. He always had, even as a small child, before the cello. He could remember his father once joking — some joke — that in a past life someone must have done something horrible to his hands.

If Keith kept his gaze forward and down, to the safe middle of the boat, he beheld another danger, and its certainty swamped his stomach: the cases of beer, the barely concealed whiskey bottle, the amber sloshing in its neck. He would be feeling awful on the return trip and there was no way out of it. He had never escaped his brothers' fun. Once the motor cut, there would be endless roaring talk. It felt like the hangover had already begun.

They looked to be about halfway from the mainland to Savory Island. They'd originally planned to rent kayaks for the crossing and do a bare-survival weekend — dried food, jig fish, poncho for a tent and all the rest of it — but thank christ Phil's back had gone out, making kayaks impossible. So this twelve-foot aluminum cartop instead, the small engine pushing it alarmingly well. It was Raymond's brother-in-law's boat so Raymond drove, and with a captain's smugness, though his steering on departure had been anything but smooth. The calm sea was fortunate because in a violent mockery of their initial intentions to rough it they'd loaded the boat with a family canvas tent, campstove, sleeping bags, coats, the booze, and an immense cooler filled with meat. So much for a little jigged fish.

Yet Keith couldn't deny it was a gorgeous day, not a cloud. Savory Island approached fresh green in the distance with its bottom rim of white, its endless beach. It was the kind of day that made you pick up your head and take that self-conscious special breath.

Keith had noticed his brothers' smiles and how the word 'fabulous' got repeated. As usual they were pushing it. Couldn't they see that by *talking* about it they lessened it? He filed away the idea that someday it would be good to come back in a kayak, alone.

"Keith! It's paradise!" Raymond shouted at him over the engine. Keith turned, nodded and smiled.

"Keith! Isn't this *paradise*?"

Keith made bug eyes and nodded absurdly. He hadn't meant to be quite so insolent. Raymond waved him away and looked at Phil and Phil shook his head. Keith, he could imagine them asking, don't you like *anything*? And he could honestly say back, I like everything, everything except people. How could you say this without insulting whoever you were talking to? And as if they didn't know it already. He supposed their relationship could be put in this nutshell: he was still trying to be left alone, and they were still trying to help change him.

They slowed, coasted, nosed into sand, then dragged the boat out of high tide's reach. Keith sat on a bleached log to watch his brothers' enthusiastic taking stock, their joyous appraisal of their whereabouts. Sand, trees, a vista, atonal waves dashing, sighing. It had them as gleeful as men in their late forties could be, and on the constant verge of shouting. They would have been hopping around had they been able. They looked ready to start building sand castles and driftwood forts.

"Smell that smell?" Raymond had turned to him while taking another smiling, exaggerated sniff. "Smell that?"

Keith, already aware of the seaweed, dutifully took a breath. "Nice."

"Great, eh?"

"It is."

"We'll get shit on your hands yet."

Keith nodded and smiled lamely as he put his hands pro-tectively behind his back, amazed to see himself do so. He hadn't heard that one in a while and it sounded not only incongru-ous but a little dangerous for a high school principal and father of three to have said it. Let's get shit on the cellist's hands. Let's swear in paradise. Let's fall to juvenilia because that's what you do when the recess bell rings.

After they unloaded the boat and stashed everything above the high tide logs, Phil did build himself something, an elabo-rate seat that was combination pit-in-the-sand and wooden back-rest, from which to drink scotch and take in the scenery. He claimed to have made it orthopaedically sound for his back. When he first sat in it with his plastic cup of scotch he went silent. Keith thought that, just maybe, a respectful meditation had descended, until his brother declared, "It's *paradise*. It's just like —" a cheap pause "— it's just like one huge TV screen." He smiled knowingly for Raymond, in effect a wink, then turned the smile on Keith with something of a challenge in it. Keith turned away, instantly tired.

He busied himself with the tent, with getting their bags and gear straight, whose was whose. He stood to eat some trail mix. Perhaps he should just dive into the booze himself, get it over with, chemical jollity being maybe the way to endure this. The sun was hot overhead, his brothers were hatless and looking a little big-eyed and lunatic already, searching for things to bark about.

Relieved to think up a popular task for himself, and one that would give him a break, Keith announced he was "heading off down to that creek to try 'n' get the beer cold." And off he headed, case of beer dangling from either hand, doubting that the distant silver trickle would be much cooler than the sea, or the air for that matter.

"Wait wait wait." Raymond ran after him, all brow-knit concern, so clumsy in the sand he ran like a hunchback. He held high a plastic cup brimming with and spilling scotch. Keith let him catch up. Out of breath, Raymond stood in front of Keith, barring his way.

"Open." Breathing hard, he held the cup to Keith's mouth. "C'mon. Open. Need some, fuel for the hike."

Keith opened.

IT CAME ALL IN A RUSH, THE SHOUTED INSTRUCTIONS, THE painful breaking camp, all grimace and moans and hangover and regret, and now this hell of the boat trip back. Phil, screaming, his back igniting every time the boat slammed a wave. Keith sat in the bow this time, getting soaked with spray, his job being to spot logs. He'd already been yelled at for not watching hard enough, for briefly turning around to rest and simply stare at his feet — the logs hide in troughs he was informed, or rather shouted at, also the tide was something so the waves were something worse because of it. Watching was a straining hell and he was getting wetter, which meant the waves were getting higher. The wind had blown off his Tilley hat right at the beginning and Raymond hadn't even considered going back for it. They weren't yet halfway. None of this could penetrate his headache or his thirst.

The soakings did wake him up to memories of last night, to

its beginnings at least. It had begun with him walking off alone again, more scotch in hand, aimlessly toeing the tide pools for signs of skittering life, brothers yelling inanities in the distance. Dinner was ready, some kind of manly gothic stew, "wolf's broth" they were calling it, slurring on purpose. It had been funny, for heading back he smelled something truly foul in the air, and gave wide berth to a rank lump that could've been the remains of a human but of course was a seal. The last sign of its spirit, he'd mused, was this smell, a smell rich enough to sicken him but ambrosia to untold armies of worming creatures with cravings much ruder than his. He remembered wishing for something to carry some rotten seal, bring it back as an offering for the stew. And he remembered nearing his brothers and pulling down his shorts and urinating where he stood, no hands, thinking they might enjoy this. But then he'd pivoted to point away from his brothers because suddenly it felt too uncomfortable not to. And suddenly a gull wheeled at his shoulder and he'd hunched and turned away from it too — but he'd smiled seeing himself do this.

The swilling and the laughter, he remembered its tempo and pitch, but laughter at what, he didn't know. He did remember them laughing about tomorrow's coming pain, about the three worst hangovers in the history of the world — ha ha ha — then more whiskey straight from the bottle. He had laughed himself at times. He remembered the running naked down the beach and into the water, the three of them chickening out at thigh level, the water numbingly cold, then yelling and breathless simply to stand there. He only barely recalled the curses and lamentations upon discovering they'd drunk themselves dry, a huge amount of booze, surprising even his brothers, who were proud but also

genuinely dismayed. And of course he remembered Phil screaming after falling over the log, his back going out completely and
severely, then he and Raymond carrying and dropping and carrying their poor brother to his sleeping bag, Phil screaming and
laughing and swearing all in one tearful frenzy.

This morning Phil was unable to walk or even move much, and
a storm was coming. Then discovering they had no water, let alone
beer, to drink. Raymond, captain, made an instant decision.

Catching a big wave's spray in the face, Keith turned around
briefly to look once more at Phil lying in the centre of the boat,
bouncing on the heaped dirty cushion of tent and food and life
jackets, all of which they'd more or less heaved in. Keith had
tried to put his life jacket on, but stopped at Phil's look.

Keith had never been this hungover. An urgency from the
pit of his body insisted that water would fix him, cold clear
water in gulps. He'd wanted to stumble off to the little creek
before helping launch the boat, but Raymond claimed to know
that the wind was rising and announced that it was now or
never. Forbidding him, in fact, from getting a drink.

Raymond had been correct about the wind. Keith didn't
know if they were in actual danger. The waves were growing.
Raymond steered squinting into the wind, looking angry and
worried. He kept the throttle at half speed. Keith didn't know
to what extent this was a measure of safety or an attempt to
keep Phil from screaming there from his big soggy pillow as the
boat's bow banged down upon each next wave. Keith only
wanted some water, and the noise to stop, his brothers' endless damn noise: one's yelling, the other's engine roar. All last
night it had been the same, one boorish blurt after another,

when all he craved was solitude and the teasing jazz of the simple snapping fire. He had gone along with their noise, had got their sophomoric shit on his hands, drank himself into idiocy, and here he was suffering the consequences, living the other side of the equation. His brothers noisier than ever. He didn't ever want to see them again.

A big wave pounded the right bow and drenched him. A wave almost as big approached and when it hit he closed his eyes and opened his mouth to catch some, its salty cool being better than nothing. He swallowed a bit and the short relief was fine. He opened his eyes just before they hit the submerged log which, as predicted, had been hiding in a trough.

As the boat rose sideways and threw them, as the log travelled the boat's length and ripped the motor from the transom, as he pitched into the water and felt the whole-body shock of it, Keith recognized this extreme slow motion and its full silence, knew he had been in danger before, or in this state before, some other time. He didn't go all the way under; his head was up and he saw the airborne boat descending on him, saw how he moved his hand away to protect it even as the metal edge came down.

THERE WAS A SENSATION OF WAKING UP, THOUGH HE'D NOT been aware of a gap in consciousness. Under water. He knew he'd been stunned, but stunned awake. Indeed, his whole being resonated a profound base E. But beyond sound. For silence was the biggest thing, was the container. He saw a brother's dim, kicking feet. It wasn't as cold as it had felt at first plunge, in fact it was body temperature. He could see perfectly into the distance now, and anything he wanted to see was there, and he didn't have to open his eyes. As soon as he accepted these surprise comforts, all began to change, to grow. He felt fine, then better than fine, then better than that, as fast as he could become aware of it. The sum of all comforts he'd known and was able to know had collected in a supremely shining focus that was too much for his size. Now he was bursting forth in all directions.

As soon as he tried to find his bearings, to find ground, which was to doubt the expanding course he was on, the guiding lights began. These were fine and helpful at first. Some were so bright they seemed a command, and though they felt necessary he had to look away. Then soft blue ones rose, pleasantly beckoning, in the near distance. He was thirsty for them. His moving to them felt smooth and good, but whenever he reached one he felt that his shining splendour had lessened and also that he had not reached the light at all, for there it was in the distance still, but changed. Softer still, and more eager for his thirst. Here the frightening ugliness started, and thus started the panic, panic so jagged and fast he had no time to remember where he'd just been or how good it had been in comparison to where he was now. The shrieking faces had all the shapes of thirst, and they were killing him, in all the ways he could be killed, their spearing and tearing backed and pushed by a shrieking poisonous chorus of noise, and it was only by fainting into a pit of possibly quenching light that he managed to escape. But the faces always found him and what they put him through was always deserved, until he fainted away again. This went on for mindless time, and the shape it all took felt like the truth of gravity, and falling.

Burning and dry, he was almost gone. What was left of him heard the sound of rushing water. He could hear that it was cold and fresh. He could see two people in bed, a man and a woman, and they were polite, and quiet with each other even as they moved, with the sound of the glorious rushing stream coming in their window. That he could not understand the language they spoke was especially attractive, their speech entering his ear as ornament instead of intrusion. An old violin on a special stand occupied a corner of their room in the well-kept manner of a shrine. The house was otherwise large and cool and empty of the noise of anyone else, so he went down into it.

HE NEVER LEARNED TO LIKE IT WHEN HIS PARENTS TALKED, either to each other or to him. The guttural "auch" of his mother's berating seemed incongruous as her gentle fingers combed down his wet hair down before she sent him off to kindergarten.

As a rule he played by himself, turning his back on whatever friend they found for him. This he did deliberately and with a smile, fully seeing himself do it. He also knew his parents were troubled whenever he ran in, screaming, from any wind. Their unease he assuaged with his violin playing; he could see their pride when they ushered in neighbours, then music teachers, to watch their young boy play so well. These teachers would nod their heads and frown surprise, and talk with his parents in muted tones in the dining room, but otherwise leave him content within himself, which was the point of music. At night he would lie awake in his room with his constant headache and listen to the sound of the stream as it made him thirstier, and as soon as his parents slept he would tread softly the length of the oak hall and run the faucet until it became cool as possible. Then he would bend to it, and drink and drink and drink.

A FOREST PATH

*The cougar was waiting for me part way up a maple tree
in which it was uncomfortably balanced ...*
— Malcolm Lowry, "The Forest Path to the Spring"

U NLIKE THE ABOVE EPIGRAPH, this is not a fiction. I have a distrust, a fear, a hatred of fiction, and I have my reasons. You might find these reasons colourful. The first example I'll give should suffice: my middle name is Lava, this the result of having had an eccentric and literary lush for a mother.

I have things to say on other subjects, but this has primarily to do with Malcolm Lowry, Dollarton's most famous man. You'll find I can speak with authority here, one of my credentials being that I grew up not more than one hundred yards from Dollarton Beach, the very place Lowry had his shack, wrote *Under the Volcano*, lived with M—, drank himself cat-eyed, and all the rest. As concerning all famous people, one hears contradictory "facts."

The first "fact" is this. It is said that Lowry's first shack, containing his only complete draft of *Volcano*, all his possessions, et cetera, was accidentally consumed by fire. It is said he was consequently overcome with despair but proceeded, using his vast reserves of memory and imagination, to write an improved draft. None of this is correct.

The true facts are that, one, in a drunken rage, his feet bandaged, Lowry burned his shack on purpose, having cut his feet too many times on the broken glass that glittered all around it. He was in the habit of disposing of his empty gin bottles out a window with but a flick of the wrist and, you see, it was time to relocate. (If you want proof, bus fare to Dollarton will give you proof. The glass is still there, and children still cut their feet.) And, fact two: while a draft of *Volcano* was destroyed, it was a draft that embarrassed him. The three other drafts were scattered around the parlors of Dollarton's sparse literati. My mother had one.

I will push on with my account now, confident that I need supply no further proof. But I should add that not only do I abstain from alcohol as resolutely as I eschew spinning fictions, I hold no tolerance for those who indulge in either. It amazes me that men like Malcolm Lowry are ever believed, let alone admired, at all. When, head in hands, he announced that morning to the various fishermen, neighbours, and squatters, "My god, my home is gone! My book is burned! But at least M— and I are alive!" he no doubt looked wretched and despairing. To be fair, how could his audience have known the truth? It was easy for Lowry to look wretched and despairing when he was in fact hungover and ashamed. But I have to ask, Why would anyone ever believe one whose profession was to weave yarns on paper? One who tried to lie and lie well? One whose voice all day was but a dry run for grander lies spawned with purple ink later that night in the name of art? Add to that his drinking. Lowry was incapable of telling the truth. Perhaps I should feel sorry for him. I don't.

While living in Dollarton, Lowry wrote a story, "The Forest Path to the Spring." It was published posthumously, by M—.

The story is a rather long, rambling affair, and while some of it is a lie, much of it is not, and so I recommend it to those who must read. In fact, it is perhaps the closest Lowry came to not lying, for the mistruths found in it are not so much lies per se as they are drunken inaccuracies. It'd like to rectify some of them.

The story involves his life in Dollarton, his life on the beach with the inlet fronting him and the dripping coastal forest pressing at his back. I find it a very nostalgic experience each time I read it, and I have read it many times. (Again, I have my reasons.) Lowry describes the unfurling of sword ferns, the damp promise of a forest at sunrise. The dutiful tides of Indian Arm, the rich, fish-rank croaks of gulls and herons, the smell of shattered cedar, the sacred light in a dewdrop reflecting the sun, the mysterious light in a dewdrop reflecting the moon. He describes creeks and trails I myself know well. He dived off rocks that I and my friends once used for the same purpose. And, more, he mentions in passing the elementary school I attended as a child (where no one knew my middle name); he describes the tiny café where I bought greasy lunchtime fries for a dime after having thrown away one of my mother's inedible eccentric sandwiches.

Again, it is a rambling story, its focus hard to find. Love, perhaps. He tells of his love for midnight walks through the forest, his love for fetching crystal mountain water from the spring, his love of dawn plunges off his porch, his love of M—, his love of life. We know that last one is a bald lie. He hated life, which is why he drank, and why he created a lying life on paper. In any case, the story's climax of sorts occurs one fateful day in the woods when a cougar leaps out of a tree across his path. He is startled, awestruck, petrified. And in what amounts to a none other than cosmic revelation he learns that his Eden, his forest haven-of-a-life, has on its outer edges forces of amorality and destruction. He discovers, it seems for the first time, that a rose has thorns. Critics cluck like sympathetic hens and suggest that what we have here is a classic hidden theme, one which reveals no less than a genius admitting to a suicidal battle with the bottle.

The cougar! What a bitter laugh! All of it!

Before I explain why I am laughing, I want to discuss my mom. Rather, memories of my late mother. Her name was Lucy, and she was unmarried. If there are two kinds of eccentric — one who doesn't try to be eccentric, and one who does — my mother was the latter. People tend to dislike her kind, withdrawing from their reek of fakery. And since my mother's kind choose their eccentricities, their choices tend to be exaggerations of qualities they admire. Mom, for instance, wanted to be a mad poet. At the start, she was neither, and by the end she was only mad.

In Dollarton in the forties it was most unattractive to dress up in flour sacks, mauve scarves, bangles, and canary-yellow hats. To spout bad poetry in public was abhorrent. This was Mom's choice. Dollarton was at the time a huddled collection of sulking fishermen and poor squatters, and though my mother had a captive audience she had few fans. Perhaps they could smell her self-consciousness; perhaps they noticed her eyes lacked that electrified blankness of the true eccentric. And while you may think what you want of her, she was but the tactless extrovert, a bucolic extension of the loud woman in the turquoise kaftan, and harmless. The harm set in when she began drinking. I see one cause of her drinking to be identical to that of that man who lived one hundred yards down the beach from her: an over-active imagination and no appreciative fans. For Lowry was at that time in no way famous.

I gather these facts from years of researching my personal history. My sources are the aforementioned fishermen and squatters. When they speak of my mother they speak kindly but apologetically. They hadn't liked her, and I can see in their faces their embarrassment. I am tempted to ease their pain and tell them I not only didn't like her much either, I detested her. And loved her, in the intense and awful way reserved for only sons. To illustrate: not long after she died I tried to read her poetry, and while I read for only ten minutes, I hyperventilated for twenty. It was dreadful poetry, revealing an embarrassing mind. But only I who loved her so much have the right to hate her so much.

I don't know if Lowry liked my mother or not. I have gathered that it was she who took to him first, if he took to her at all. She must have seen him there on Dollarton Beach, looking shyly Slavic-eyed, yet burping and twitching like a lunatic in the hot noon sun. He would have been as naked as legally possible, for in the early days he was proud of his build. Mother would have known he was a writer. She must have thought: At last! Another sparkling mind! I believe she first tried to attract his attention in the local bar, where it's reported she attempted (successfully) to buy him drinks. I don't know what M——, secure in her childlike love for him, must have made of that. And it's said she would sometimes flag him down in the streets, the trails, on the beach. Perhaps she'd borrow a canoe and arrange to accidentally bump bows out on the inlet. I can picture her trying to impress him. My spine creeps as I envision her passing a lime-green scarf over her unblinking Mata Hari gaze. Having caught his eye, my mother now goes for his mind and, with that flaccid flare of spontaneity-rehearsed-for-days, she points to the sun and cries laughing, "The moon! The moon!" (I believe my mother was capable of little more than cheap paradox. I also believe she was the last person of this century who held alliteration to be somehow profound. Not long before she died she said to me, in that awesome hoarse whisper of hers, "Meeting Malcolm melted my mind.")

I suspect that you share my embarrassment. But I would also hope you are coming to understand my loathing for imagination, and writers, and fiction, and drink. If not, keep an open mind. My sole purpose here is to free the steel blade of truth about Lowry from the paste-jeweled scabbard of fable that now hides it. I can assure you I'm not denigrating Mom here for pleasure.

So I doubt that Lowry liked my mother much, unless he was a bigger fool than I imagine. His writing demands that I admit he, unlike my mother, at least possessed subtlety. Perhaps fleeting genius; clarity in bursts (burps). Whatever the case, how my mother got hold of his manuscript is unclear. It could be that, like an adult relenting at last and giving candy to a brat, Lowry handed over a copy so she would go away. He likely thought it would take a woman like Lucy a full year to sift through such a book as *Volcano*, but he was wrong. No, in Mom's words, she "communed with his mind for twenty-three hours straight," and finished it. And her "communion" with him proved to be the beginning of her end. For my mother, whose mind's sole ambition was to snap colourfully, Lowry's fiction, his obsessive flowery pain-packed verbiage, was the necessary nudge. It was on the day following Mom's twenty-three hour binge that the Event — and my reason for writing this — took place.

The Event has to do with the story, "The Forest Path to the Spring," specifically with the cougar the narrator saw. As I mentioned, he was out collecting water from the spring, looked up, and there was the cougar. He describes the encounter at great length. Again, it was "uncomfortably balanced" in the tree. It was "caught off guard or off balance," and then "jumped down clumsily." But it was "sobered and humiliated by my calm voice" and it "slunk away guiltily into the bushes." There is more, much more. Page upon page about the cougar, Lowry's fear of it, his thoughts about his fear, his thoughts about these thoughts, his clinging passionately to M— all through the ensuing night, shaking and having tremulous sex together in the knowledge that Danger Lurks.

That cougar made quite an impression on him. However, I'd like to draw your attention to his summation of the encounter, which was that it was so weird an apparition that "an instant later it was impossible to believe he'd ever been there at all." Having done so, I'll simply come out with it: That was no cougar. That was my mom.

I SOMETIMES WONDER JUST HOW DRUNK A MAN CAN GET. I think about that as I try year by year to understand the man Malcolm Lowry.

Wandering Dollarton Beach (or Cates Park, as it's come to be called) again this week, along the path that is now proclaimed by sign to be Malcolm Lowry Walk, I took a good steady look. A sober look. I studied hard this plot of land and sea described by Lowry to be "everywhere an intimation of Paradise." He found "delicate light and greenness everywhere, the beauty of light on the feminine leaves of vine-leaved maples and the young leaves of the alders shining in sunlight like stars." Oh, he goes on and on and on. Unadulterated opulence, with four adjectives per noun. But here is the one I can't help but smile grimly at: "The wonderful cold clean fresh salt smell of the dawn air, and then the pure gold blare of light from behind the mountain pines, and the two morning herons, then the two blazing eyes of the sun over the foothills." Did you get that? *Two* suns? The words *blaring* and *blazing* to describe light? This is a description not of nature but of a raging dawn double-vision hangover. I have lived here by the beach all my life and I have never seen herons travel in pairs. This passage would have been different had the man had a palm pressed to one eye.

While walking the identical path I saw beauty too, certainly, but not Lowry's bombastic brand. I, too, saw rustling dainty foliage of one hundred shades of green. I saw sturdy stoic trees, and mountains with their awesome noble mysterious elan. (It's easy to be Lowry.) Boats on the oh-so-wonderful water, King Neptune's refreshing wavelets tickle-slapping the angel-white hulls, et cetera.

But what else did I see? I saw slugs mid-path, dry pine needles stuck to their dragging guts, their bellies torn open by the sensible shoes of strolling ladies. I saw dull clouds muffling mountains logged off and scarred forever; clouds muting the high notes of birds; clouds reflected better in the oil slicks than in the patches of clear water. I saw rotten stumps, diseased leaves, at least as much death as life. In short, I saw reality. I had no need of hiding from the truth. I didn't have the need of a man ashamed, the need of a vision hungover and in constant pain. Lowry donned his rose-coloured glasses and painted the shuffling grey world with the glad shades of Eden in order to stay sane. Art was his excuse as much as it was his tool. He probably believed what he wrote.

On to my mother, and the Event. I should add that I heard all of this straight from Mom's mouth, and the disturbing mix of anguish and ecstasy in her eyes as she spoke makes me doubt not a word of it. She told me several times, and the story didn't vary.

Her words:

"I just finished reading *Volcano*. In twenty-three hours. Oh, I was in rapture. I was under a spell. He had called out to me and I wanted to answer. And I had to answer in a worthy way. I decided to go to him dressed to celebrate the Day of the Dead. In the book this was the first thing mentioned — the Day of the Dead, the costumes, the skulls, and all of those things that so horrified poor Geoffrey Firmin. In the end Death is the last thing Geoffrey sees. It is the book's heart: Death. It was important that Malcolm knew I understood, as he knew I would. So I made the skeleton costume. The material should have been black, or course, but I had no time, and all I had was a brown one, a rabbit costume left from a bygone Hallowe'en dance. I cut off the ears and painted on the bones. It wasn't a good job, I'm afraid. My word, I had just read *Under the Volcano* and naturally my hands were shaking."

I was scared as my mother told me this part, because each time she told me, even though the Event was years past, even though Lowry was dead and Mother was in her hospital ward only obliquely aware of me, her hands would begin to shake.

"But the idea itself was enough. My plan was to show up at his door, because I knew M— was back East. She hadn't taken to me, you see, and I can't say as I blame her, of course. Malcolm would act positively fidgety around me, a torn man. But anyway I happened upon a better plan. I felt it was important that he *look up* to see me, to see Death, just as Geoffrey did at the end, from under his horse. So I climbed a tree and waited. I knew he'd be along soon. I had spied on poor Malc and I knew his habits. Englishmen, especially Englishmen who drink, have strict habits."

Here Mother would stare coyly down at her feet, pretending naughtiness, and laugh like a girl. The final time I heard this story Mom looked very old, her fingers were ochre from cigarettes, she was dressed as always (the staff let her keep her stash of scarves and hats under her bed), and yet she could giggle as pure and free as a little girl. I felt like crying. I felt like looking up and shouting: You may be dead, Mr. Lowry, but *look what you are doing.*

"So I found a nice tree and waited. And my lord don't you know I fell asleep. All that reading and no sleep. Also, I confess to having sipped some."

That is, had a lot to drink. But I admit I love to picture her up that tree, and I perversely enjoy Lowry's version, that of "a lion uncomfortably balanced." What a nobly optimistic euphemism for a snoring drunk crazy lady hanging there like a noodle on a chopstick.

"But I knew Malcolm would understand. When he gave me the book he said, in that marvelous Oxonian of his, 'This is a tome best read drunk, for so its best bits were thunk.' Ah, Malc, a lad so boyish. A boyish genius."

Here Mom might drift off. If I felt like hearing more, I'd prod.

"There I was asleep, eight feet up. The next thing I knew, I heard a scream. Yes, a scream. My lord don't you know I thought it was a woman? I must have startled, for I fell. And considering I could have met Death myself right then and there, I wasn't hurt much. A broken rib and a cut on my back, and thank the lord for having sipped some. When I looked up, there was

Malcolm running with his clattering empty water pails back in the way of his cabin. He was making the most curious noises in his throat. I was concerned. I think he'd been sipping rather heavily that week, what with you-know-who gone."

My mother's story would go on one segment longer. She would gaze searchingly through the smudged windows of years until, seeing what she wanted to see, her eyes would close and she'd say, "And I followed Malcolm Lowry home. In I walked, dressed as Death, bleeding from my back, and told him I loved him. He rose slowly from his bed, stood ramrod straight and told me in a whisper that he loved me too."

Once, and only once, she added: "And we … communed." Perhaps realizing for the first time who her audience was, Mom went instantly shy and changed the subject. My mother may have been extroverted and insane, but she was conservative when it came to certain subjects.

I SAW MALCOLM LOWRY ONLY TWICE THAT I REMEMBER. I was eight or nine, and it was just before he returned to England for good. The first time, my mother had sent me to his cabin with a letter, sealed in a black envelope and smelling — good god — of perfume. Lowry bellowed "Come!" at my knock, and there he was, sitting at his writing table. He had erect posture and a barrel chest, but a big and flabby stomach. A deeply proud bearing. His eyes looked almost Oriental. He just sat there, sober I think, and he seemed to know who I was. He didn't looked pleased to see me. I gather from my probings that during those years he'd been spending considerable energy avoiding my mother. I gave him the letter and fled.

The second time, mere weeks later, I was again a messenger boy. I knocked at the same door, and hearing only the oddest whoops and titters but no invitation to enter, I peered in at a window. There sat the same man, but hardly. This time he was naked. (I have heard he sometimes wrote that way.) He looked dark and crude, a greasy feline-eyed peasant. His table was littered with papers and books, and crumpled balls of foolscap covered his cabin floor like a spill of giant's popcorn. He was hunched over and rolls of pale fat lay on his lap. He began to make noises again, noises that are unforgettable but hard to describe: a high-pitched kind of squealing, but with a deep bass undertone at the same time. As he squealed he swung his head back and forth in arcs. His lips were clamped open, showing teeth, and his scrunched eyes looked on the verge of tears — like he was trying for tears. Swinging his head faster and faster, he finally stopped and took several glugs from a bottle he had at hand's reach on the floor. I recognized the brand: Bols, the same English gin my mother drank. I stared, fascinated, with the avid hollowness of car accidents when a cop with a flashlight stands over a puddle of someone's blood. What made me run in the end was this: Lowry finally managed to get a pipe lit after missing the bowl with several matches. He took a long draw and settled back and sighed as if in satisfaction. But instead he grew dizzy from the smoke. He began to sway in his chair. And suddenly he shot up, threw back his head and howled. In the middle of howling — I swear this is true — he accidentally shit himself. I *think* it was an accident. In any case it was an explosion of diarrhea, expelled in a one-second burst. Much of it sprayed his buttocks and legs and, snarling now, Lowry began to twirl and slap at the wetness, stumbling as he did so. I ran then.

I realize I am more or less trampling on the reputation of a man a good many readers respect and admire. And I don't mean to rub it in further — no, I only mean to establish thoroughly my reasons for writing this — when I tell you it was on the same afternoon that I first heard Malcolm Lowry was a famous man. Handing me her latest note, Mother had told me, "Be careful with this, Dear, you are taking it to a very special person. He is a writer, and his book is in all the bookstores of the world." Well, I had just seen my first writer, my first famous man, and now fame and fiction had a face.

You have already guessed a number of things. First, the reason for my bitterness — namely, that Lowry and my mother had sex after she fell from the tree. My feelings stem not so much from the act itself but rather because what meant so much to my mother meant so little to Lowry. I believe it was his utter rejection of her after the Event that shoved her down insanity's slide.

Mother never told me about it herself, this I admit, but the evidence pointing to their carnal union is overwhelming and I don't for a moment doubt it took place. One, she told me she followed him back. Two, M— was away. Three, as she told me but once, they "communed." And my research has given me these clues as well: There was a two week period during M—'s absence when Lowry was purportedly most upset. "Crazy," my sources put it. On a non-stop gin binge, he raved to all who'd listen that he'd met Death in the flesh, that he'd met Death and defeated it. One barfly heard him distinctly say, "I rogered Death from behind like a dog." (I don't like to picture this.) During that period of time he would laugh and rave, rave and cry. What ended his raving was news of a cougar in the area.

Hearing this news seemed to cheer him up. He took to saying he too had seen the cat, and so his run-in with Death went the way of bad dreams. It takes no detective to sort out the self-serving machinations of this drunken man's mind. For sanity's sake, for relief from devils, he made himself believe he'd seen a cougar, not my mother, not Death.

I hate but can't help picturing the scene. Lowry, drunk and whimpering, finds that Death has not only leapt at him from a tree but has followed him to his door. My mother, ludicrous in a rabbit's costume with a skeleton etched on it, with a broken rib and bleeding from the back, tells him she loves him. She embraces him and, scared, Lowry can't deny Death its desire. My mother instigates the unthinkable. And two hideously incongruous dream worlds unite there in a shack on Dollarton Beach: My mother believing she has won over her aloof treasure, her boyish genius. Lowry believing he is copulating with Death.

On Lowry's behalf, I like to assume that at some point in his passion he reached that minimal level of awareness where he realized it was in fact a mortal woman in his bed. Someone who was not M——. Though in "The Forest Path to the Spring" he writes that after his brush with the cougar he and M—— "embraced all the night long," I should restate that during this time M—— was gone for three months, and I doubt that even a gin-riddled Lowry could stay unaware of that. So did he know it was my mother? Did he make himself believe it was M——? What shaped pretzel of logic did he construct in order to stay sane? Lowry was by all accounts a monogamous husband, and so perhaps it was his horror at this odd adultery that made him go mad for a while. We'll never know.

For years, my mother assumed he'd known it was her. But when she first learned of his death — she did not read newspapers and it was me who told her — she said, "I thought he'd send word. *Some*thing." Then she laughed, and lapsed back into what was now her world, a state of waking dream. And when "The Forest Path to the Spring" came out in 1960, and after Mother read certain parts over and over, she closed the book at last and — cried.

I could go on and on about Lowry's life, Lowry's lies to himself. Indeed, I could water my prose with imagination and assault the man with a decadently flowery language he would well have recognized. It is tempting. I see now how the taking up of a pen and the posture of writing itself seem to abet some kind of exaggeration. Once begun, words find their own momentum in the direction of colour, veneer, dream. Lie. I can only hope that by now you understand that my loathing for fiction is so resolute it has allowed me during this account to tell you nothing but the granite truth. However much I am tempted to sink into venom, attach the leash of speculation to Lowry's name and drag it through any number of cesspools, I won't.

Nor will I go on to describe his final fall, for to do so would be to ennoble it. His tawdry death. Myth be damned: his death was nothing but tawdry, as tawdry as my mother's. I'll draw no cheap conclusion from this, but the equation is there for all to see: two people, lashed by self-doubt, forced by life's grinning skull to turn to dreams and poetry and imagination, poisoned yet further by alcohol — two people die a false and tawdry death. My point is made. I give it to you and leave it; I ask only that you refrain from embellishing either their lives or their deaths with yet more poetry. I have the right to ask this.

I'll likely never discover whether Lowry knew he was my father. He may have known; he may only have guessed. Perhaps Mom told him. Perhaps she pestered. But, not being the kind to ask for money or seek a scandal, my mother would have preferred cherishing me in secret, me her precious relic of a single sacred meeting.

Not knowing has been hard on me. Harder, in fact, than having had no taste of fatherhood, save for a singular image of a naked man squealing, stumbling, slapping at glistening legs. It's been hardest of all to admit to myself that, in the booze-blurred moment of my conception, not only was I not planned, not sought for, but was in fact the result of a man's lust for a woman other than my mother. To be blunt, Lowry's sperm was meant for M——(or perhaps for Death!), but was waylaid, like a manuscript, by a lonely woman in a bid for a bit of attention. Such was the flavour of my beginning, and such remains the flavour of my life.

Proof that I'm his son? It took no wizardry to ascertain the year and month of the cougar Event, add to it nine months and, lo and behold, arrive at my birthday. My mother had no boyfriends and was not known to have affairs. Lucy was a remarkable woman in many ways, not the least of which being that she knew a man's nakedness but once, and this while wearing a rabbit costume.

As I mentioned when I began, my middle name is Lava. "The Forest Path to the Spring," and the later stories — and according to my mother, all his work-to-come — were to be part of a magnum opus he would call *Mount Appetite*, a renaming of

Mount Seymour, the mountain at whose foot Dollarton squats. Why rename a mountain? For poetry's manipulative sake, of course. For metaphor's aggrandizements. According to Mom, Lowry raved about his project endlessly and famously, to all who would listen. People here talk of it still. *Mount Appetite* was to catalogue and sanctify the many kinds of human desire. A portrait of passions, a rainbow of hungers. (Gamut of gluttonies. I can't help but picture a troupe of pained eccentrics, driven by desires feral, pungent, twisted and hidden. Equipped with ropes and spiked boots and clenched jaws they eternally scale the Sisyphian heights of their sticky needs.)

My mother's inspiration for "Lava" was equally metaphoric, if sillier. In this case, I know the meaning. In her way of speaking to me as though I weren't there, staring up into space and talking over my head both literally and figuratively, Mother more than once intoned grandly, "Lava. You are my Lava. My dear little man. You are the emission of a volcano."

She doubtless imagined I'd be as wordproud as my father. No. But I'll travel that road as long as I can stomach and extend her metaphor for her: hot lava is upchucked dumbly into the world, soon cools, and resents having been spewed there. Lava is nothing like the fiery bowels of its father. If lava could feel, it would feel like effluent, like scum. Not art but puke. It would feel carelessly and wrongfully ejaculated — I cannot resist — under the volcano.

As I've been writing this history, I've often stopped and asked myself: Is this the voice of bitterness? Malc and Lucy's bitter bastard boy? If not, why do I smear both a mother and a father? I seek neither notoriety nor a noble name, neither a paternity suit nor a share of his estate, if he left one. So why do I expose? Whose voice is this?

I like to think it is my father's voice — his voice had he lived, his voice had he learned to stop lying, had he learned to lift his head high and breathe for good and all the pure cold air of objectivity. If children inherit one thing from their parents it is the claustrophobic fear of their parents' faults. I thank mine for helping me, through revulsion, toward clarity. My mind's best food has been the flesh of their faulty lives. Neither of my parents understood that appetite is mostly about the art of control.

I've been drunk but once in my life. I was seventeen. My mother had just died. That it happened to be my high school graduation party didn't matter to me — this wasn't a celebration but an exorcism. We drank under the stars in — where else? — Dollarton Beach. Under Mount Appetite. In paradise. A body had been found here in a burned-out car earlier that week, a murder, so added to the evening was an air of danger lurking. And I drank gin, my parents' brand. I slept with neither cougar, ghost, nor woman, but still I had a wondrous time. I cried about my mother and raged about my father, pounding a driftwood club into the beachfire, sending showers of glowing amber skyward. None of the other kids noticed me really, for many were on a first-drunk as well, and flailed about in their own style and for their own reasons.

MARIA'S OLDER BROTHER

"HEEEEYYYYY, CUT!"

Never failed to suck Tony in. There he was, swinging blindly at the third pitch in a row. The other team yelling "cut" would mix him up; he'd obey instead of defy. They'd go wild, jeering and laughing their heads off, as if they'd never seen him do it before. He'd done it several times in this same game. We made a normal enough scene. No doubt some would have seen us as a perfect Norman Rockwell: kids red and hairblown in the sun, the kid shouts, the loose clothes and healthy dirt, the big safe sky and green grass. But I remember us being more real than that. There was fear and hate and the frantic will to win. I know there were also young worries, but I can't recall why, or what about. Perhaps the sky was safer than now.

Here came Jacky Adams, running to the field with his glove, pulling off his coat, his mouth swollen from the dentist. We could kick Tony off our team now. It was an important game, tied, and late in the season. Summer holidays were starting soon, which meant the teams would be split up as parents dragged kids with them to this or that lake.

We all waited for Tony to start walking off the field, head down, glove off, without being told. He knew he was supposed to. Not even his sister's dying could hold him on the team. It should have been a simple formality. Jacky Adams should have taken over his position easily, an obvious exchange of the body that belonged for the body that didn't. We wanted to play.

It was the last time we played baseball that spring. As for me, I haven't played since. Our parents, worried after what happened, took many of us to the lake earlier that year. As if what Tony had done was infectious.

I don't know if we were ever told what Maria died of; if we were I can't remember it. She must have been ten at the time, the same as most of us. She was also in Mrs. Evers' class at school (it was called the Young Road Elementary School — I didn't see the contradiction or humor in this name until much later).

Maria had been away most of May and June. I can picture Tony, Maria's older brother, coming wild-eyed to school one morning two weeks before summer holidays, saying, "My sister died yesterday. No one could wake her up." He said this over and over, turning to anyone who was listening. All of us were, of course, so his head was jerking this way and that. He also said, over and over, "My parents wanted me to go to school anyway!" Two years older than his sister, Tony was in the same class as well.

Hearing of death didn't affect us the same way it does adults. We somehow ran free of death's absolute gravity and weren't thrown into any kind of lasting brood when we heard of someone dying. We got stuck only in the real changes, ruptures in the flow of the day. Everyone's known a Leslie K, who, after missing a week of school, returns one morning but doesn't talk, won't smile, and goes straight home, having that mysterious disease called "her father died." It would be the changed Leslie who made us nervous, and not her invisible father and his unknowable death. We took nothing of dying home with us. Maria was away for good, and we had to rearrange science partners.

It was in keeping with Tony to announce his sister's death as he would have his father's new car. Though we had no words for it, we were repelled by his trying to use Maria as a social lever, to put himself in the class's eye. He was after momentary stardom, and we knew that he was going a little too far here, stepping sloppily over some barrier even kids recognize.

But there was also the black thought — suddenly becoming a guilty thought, I don't know why — of Maria in the big culvert pipe in Dollarton. It was my first lusty event, though innocent enough. Nervous kisses, doctor games, shocking vulva. Already I would wince at the memory, perhaps because Maria was so shy and trusting. Word of her death in some way complicated guilt. I'm not sure if Tony knew of the episode, or even if he would have cared.

It was natural for Tony to want to belong, but he was one of those unfortunates who never would, having nothing of value to offer. He made matters worse by trying to imitate us, shamelessly eager and in over-obvious ways. The way we'd posture in the back row, which of the teacher's jokes we condescended to laugh at, the words we'd use to pick on a girl. Tony's looks made his attempt doubly pathetic. He was the archetypal kid who'd failed a few times, was the biggest in class, the first to get pimples, was growing clumsier and flabbier at the same time, had greasy hair too long and hanging at the front, a chipped tooth and a stupid but crazed — glassy — animal look in his eyes. So Tony's imitations were grotesque.

His idol was Bobby Horton — blond, angelic, probably the best peewee hockey player in North Vancouver. Tony's dog-loyalty and his struggles at emulating Bobby, at trying to walk and talk like the perfect Canadian boy, make a sad memory, but it wasn't sad at the time: we were kids, and when kids laugh at someone they laugh with pure appetite, like devils.

Too bad Tony wasn't a good athlete like Bobby Horton. Or even passable like the rest of us. You could be the biggest misfit in the world but if you could beat the throw to first or make the odd diving catch you could assume your fair place in the schoolyard pecking order.

Also it was a plus to be "dumb in school." But only if you could manage an air that you could do it easily if only you felt like trying. Tony was certainly "dumb in school," and even copied our attitude, but it was too plain that he was dumb and only dumb, that he'd failed already and would again. Whenever we got the strap we got it for being too daring (like the time that same spring, when Bill Cummings famously scissored off almost half the pigtail of the new girl in front of him, before getting caught), but any time Tony went out in the hall to get Mrs. Evers' twenty stiff palm-whacks we knew, listening from our back-row group slouch, that he was getting it for the sole reason that he was too dumb.

I remember once Tony getting strapped for trying to be perfect. It looked like he had decided to make a day of it because he started first thing in the morning, in front of the school gate, as soon as Bobby Horton passed by on his way in. Tony had on a crisp new ball cap, black, the kind Bobby wore. He shifted his books to his right hand, carrying them carelessly, half-falling, the way Bobby did. And so on: he followed Bobby around the halls, stooping at the water fountain when Bobby finished there.

In the classroom, it got out of hand. Still trying to pour himself into this ideal mold, he copied Bobby's fidgeting, followed him once to the bathroom without being allowed, and repeated each and every thing Bobby said out loud to Mrs. Evers. It was this last thing — the restating, word for word, of Bobby's answers — that got to the teacher. To her, ten-year-old behavior had nothing to do with mental health: either you were being "good" or being "bad." Tony wasn't being good here so obviously he was being bad, copying, in his sloppy-mouthed way, Bobby Horton's good words.

So though Tony was only going crazily overboard, Mrs. Evers thought he was mocking Bobby Horton, and she strapped him for it. Bobby was too scared to intervene and explain how she had misread the affair; to do so would have been to call her stupid. Mocking takes malice and brains, and it was clear to us that Tony had neither.

No one would have intervened anyway. Tony deserved no sympathy. He had nothing at all attractive for us, so we could see no reason in the world to be friendly to him. It was as simple as that. But occasionally we had to let him play baseball with us.

I remember everything about that last game, and still see it as if magnified, and slightly surreal. I recall throwing up — and getting some of it, it was orange coloured, on my glove. Not feeling sick, just throwing up, as if to get rid of what I was seeing. Others were throwing up too. And I remember the smell of the grass and the dust on the diamond, and there were Rockwell birds still chirping in the branches behind the backstop, as if they couldn't see what was going on below.

THERE WAS ALWAYS A GAME GOING AT THE HIGH SCHOOL, which had the best diamond, with spiked-in bases, and if the bigger kids moved in to claim what was theirs we'd head to the other field in Myrtle Park, a few blocks away. There was a game every afternoon from after school until dinner-time, and marathon, all-day games on weekends. These games were serious business, probably the biggest drain on our endless kid-energy, certainly more than school. All the scores were recorded, and individual statistics kept (at least by the better players) — home runs, RBI's, stolen bases, hits — so there was competition here as well.

Tony would bring his glove to school like the rest of us, but only rarely could we let him play. The two teams were more or less set. One was called "Bobby's team" after Bobby Horton, and Ralph Steinbach was captain of "Ralph's team." Each squad had its nucleus of six or seven regulars, along with a few poorer or younger players who filled in vacancies or once in a while got to play an inning in right field. Sometimes, if the score was already lopsided by the third inning, to keep excitement alive either Bobby or Ralph would stop play to work out a trade.

The dreaded trade. Though at least an average player, I feared the day I might be picked to be "the bad player" in a trade. No one was actually called "the bad player," but it was obvious who he was. There was no question. We'd watch him walk across the field, knowing he was joining the other team for the sole purpose of being an active deficit — an albatross necklace, a predictable Jonah. Not exactly embraced by his new teammates, he'd have to accept his status quietly, or not play. There wasn't much chance of me being traded: I was Bobby Horton's best friend. Tony was traded pretty well every time he played.

Which wasn't often, but he watched every game from the sidelines nonetheless. It was more like waiting than watching, for he showed little interest in the action on the field. He'd fold himself up and sit on his glove, maybe pull grass to pick his teeth with, maybe scratch the bench with a twig. He'd get to play when some team needed a body, when someone had to leave and it was too early for us to quit. But usually, after waiting out the game to its finish, Tony would turn from the field and walk slowly away, head down, his glove bouncing off his leg in rhythm.

It made us uncomfortable to have Tony watching and waiting like he did, but it was more uncomfortable when he played. His near-worship of us and his delight at being allowed to play with younger, smaller, weaker boys was a violation of some natural law we all felt, and a little sickening to witness. Tony the sloppy goof, the crazy idiot. It was easier just to be cruel.

Several times early in the season we tried letting him, instead of someone's sister, be umpire — but Tony was so afraid of making anyone angry he could never decide on close calls. He couldn't conceive of calling a strike on anyone like Bobby Horton, as if rules were there to serve and not test kids like him. Girls were by far the best umps because they were detached enough to mediate — they weren't much bothered by the game itself, and were grateful for the attention even if it meant taking the abuse it did. But Tony caused more arguments than there would have been with no umpire at all.

We played as only kids can. The will to win was pure and unchecked. The games were wars, and our loyalty to a team was battlefield loyalty. The battle was fiercest during arguments. Kids indulging the game fantasy to its utmost: each moment in the game was where we lived and where we died. During crisis moments within this little lifetime we would scream an insane "HE WAS SAFE!" while all that was evil in the world threw up a wall of voices: "HE WAS OUT! HE WAS OUT! HE WAS OUT!" A close call at home plate would without fail bring on the gut-contest, the head-to-head screaming match. (The umpire, standing well off to the side and ignored, knew now that she had been nothing but an ornament all along.) Even lesser reasons — a hit that maybe was foul — would see us raging at each other, the loser condemned to hell. I recall the straining necks with small veins bulging.

These arguments were common, going on and on and on, and they would sometimes end the game altogether. If an argument seemed endless either Ralph or Bobby, whoever felt more cheated and righteous, would collect his players and make to leave with them. At this threat the other leader would have to intervene, and in a wise, slightly bored voice, save the day but at the same time kill it by announcing, "It doesn't matter … it's only a game." It didn't matter. The waving arms and shouting would drop, the eyes film over a little; gloves would be put back on and the ball returned to the pitcher. The game was dead for a while, kids making that reluctant leap into an adult world which sees life as the largest thing and games as games, that don't matter. In fact, this leap became the new contest, the new game. It was a game no one wanted to play; but once someone started it — *It doesn't matter, it's only a game* — the plug was pulled and you played it whether you wanted to or not.

Keeping Tony out of the games was clumsy and cruel enough on its own. His sister dying made it touchier, pushing on us feelings we couldn't identify. If any of our better friends had had a sister die it might have brought sympathy at first and then a respect, a kind of odd status. But Maria's death made Tony stranger still, a stupid sad-boy who deserved our hate even more. He wrecked the purity of our game.

BUT ON THAT DAY, DURING THE IMPORTANT GAME TIED LATE in the eighth inning, with Jacky Adams running onto the field still numb from the dentist, Tony had so far played the entire game, planted in right field like a bent stick. And though normally he would have left without challenging being thrown out, today he wouldn't leave. Jacky Adams ran up near him, put on his glove, pulled his cap out of his back pocket, but Tony wouldn't budge. He stood where he was without acknowledging Jacky at all.

Everyone on both teams was chattering and more anxious still because Jacky was back. A good hitter (certainly way better than Tony, who would have been up soon), he gave an extra edge to our chances. We were all eager and shouting to get the game going again — and then we noticed Tony stooped out there in right field.

"C'mon, let's go!"

"Hey Tony! C'mon, Jacky's playing!"

"*C'mon!*"

He stayed. Not knowing what else to do, Jacky took up a position next to him, pounded his glove a couple of times and went into the fielder's stance, bent over with hands on knees, focused on home plate and the next batter. The shouting grew. Tony reached into his pocket, got out a stick of gum, unwrapped it, put it into his mouth, and then bent down in readiness too, staring straight ahead, obstinate, chewing.

Bobby Horton, who was pitching and on the verge of maybe striking out their team's best batter, was more impatient than the rest of us. He waved Tony away, growing furious, shouting: "C'mon! Get off the field! Jacky's back!" Tony stared straight ahead. Bobby Horton yelled again: "*Get the hell off!*" He paused for a moment. Then he yelled once more, very distinctly, very slowly:

"Go-play-with-your-sister!"

It hit us all like a sickening blow. From what I had heard my parents say, I knew that Maria was still at her house, "lying in state," and I had too clear a picture of the Rizzuto home, the right upstairs window and a ghostly form lying on a bed.

We wished it hadn't been said, however much it was in some way fitting. But it was said, and everyone could only go quiet to see what Tony did. He didn't do much of anything. He gave Bobby Horton a long, blank look (I thought they might fight — fighters have that same empty look) but then he abruptly turned away and ran home. We watched this, but not for long. We were playing again in seconds. And Jacky Adams caught the fly ball hit to him, justifying all.

I remember everything clearly. It happened maybe ten minutes later, after we had retired their side and Bobby Horton was up to bat. It was a crucial situation. The score was tied, the game was in the last inning. I was on deck and with two out I wondered if I would get up again. Bobby had to get a hit. I knew he would. He had the look. He was going to be mean with the ball.

"Heeeeyyyyy, CUT!" Bobby swung so hard at the first one he put himself off balance and missed widely. The next pitch was a ball. Then another ball, but just — a small argument, which Ralph Steinbach generously conceded. Bobby hit the next pitch foul along the third base line but it made us all laugh when the third baseman tried to field it anyway and it bounced off a rock and hit him in the neck. He cried for a minute or so, which held up the game and made the tension unbearable. Two out and Bobby Horton had two strikes on him. The guys were beside themselves, fidgeting and dancing around.

Janice the umpire screamed "Maria!" before their pitcher had released the ball. Everyone had been so intent on the coming pitch, on Bobby Horton still and blond at home plate, that we had not noticed Tony coming towards us through right field from the direction of his home. What must have been his mother and several other adults were in the distance, screaming and gaining ground on him.

Tony was carrying Maria. We were frozen as he ran onto the diamond with her, heading for home pate, breathing in short, hoarse gasps. He passed the pitcher's mound at full speed. Stopping dead ten feet from where Bobby Horton stood fixed, bow-legged with raised bat, he heaved Maria into the air, roaring "Heeeeyyyyyy, CUT!"

I can see Maria in slow motion. Her face bony and white, but still Maria. Her body seemed no more than a skeleton: stick-thin and rigid, draped in a limp white dressing gown. Her hands had been folded to her chest but Tony's throw caused them to come away, at odd angles, bent like chicken wings. Maria hit the ground on home plate. Her hair, long and black, oily from sickness, spread out in a spider-halo around her head. Dust began to settle on it.

The adults had caught up. They were hysterical, out of themselves with shock, which to us was almost as unsettling as Maria there on the ground, was probably what frightened us most, what made us start to cry ourselves.

Instantly they were taking Tony and Maria away. One they grabbed roughly, the other they took up with care and with tears. The men and women around Tony screamed at him and at each other, and they were waving their arms and pulling him this way and that. I have an image of their veins, cording and straining in their necks.

It looked as if Tony wanted to come back and play. He kept struggling to look at us, and he dragged against their hold on him.

"It doesn't matter!" he shouted to them, looking from one to another, on his face a good copy of a bored sort of wisdom. "It doesn't matter!"

THE BRONZE
MIRACLE

Not surprising. He's left me with a puzzle: even after reading about him in the paper, I don't know who he is.

I MET HIM MY FIRST NIGHT ON THE JOB, AND ALMOST RUINED it by phoning the police. Ruined what? Our trust, I guess. That's what grew between us, unless I'm mistaken, unless I flatter myself. (Flatter myself. Flattered that a ten-year-old kid might like me. Some big law says it should be the other way around.)

But that first night I almost phoned the police. There I stood in my starchy red 7-Eleven uniform, my till full of change, my bat under the counter ready for drunk fights and robbers, when in from out of these dead suburbs walks a ten-year-old kid. It was two-thirty in the morning. He was short and reed-thin, with greasy black hair so long in front he kept flicking his head to see. He grabbed a Coke from #2 cold display case, opened it, threw six quarters on my counter without looking up and walked over to thumb through the comics.

I turned and watched him through the fish-eye. In the mirror's distortion he looked even more pale and pathetic. What was a kid his age doing out at this hour, drinking caffeine? (Dollarton is no New York. It's not even Saskatoon.) Was he a runaway? Shoplifter? He lacked the baggy coat or big pockets where a shoplifter would "stuff stuff," as my supervisor had instructed me just that evening. This kid wore only jeans and ratty T-shirt. Maybe he was a grab-and-runner. The longer I watched him, the more I suspected he watched me back, sideways, through his greasy strands of hair.

Ten minutes passed before he wandered over to my counter and stood before it, studying the lottery tickets under the glass. I had an eerie feeling that, though he never looked right at it, he also studied the gold filling I wear on a chain around my neck.

"A foot-long," he said, still not looking up. He had a high voice and for some reason I'd expected an adult one. Oddly, and I might be wrong, but *he* seemed to want a deep voice too, as though his perfectly normal kid-voice embarrassed him.

Waxing paternal, I felt for him. Tomorrow was a school day. I decided he had drunk parents at home fighting.

I took his money and gave him his hotdog.

"Everything okay?" I asked, trying to sound nonchalant.

He looked up then. It was as though our ages were instantly reversed. His eyes were so clear. It wasn't a sneer he gave me, but the patient look given moronic questions. I saw then that this had all been my imagination, that at no time had he looked either shoplifter-sly or upset. If anything he looked bored. As he left now, another word popped up: regal. This kid, I decided, was bored royalty. I wondered who his subjects were, and what he commanded, out here in the middle of the night.

I DIDN'T SEE THE KID FOR SEVERAL NIGHTS RUNNING AND forgot about him, busy as I was learning the ropes, as they say. In the world of midnight 7-Eleven these ropes are a thudding mix of neon and monotonous. Though I never did actually thank heaven for the place, it wasn't too bad a job, as bad jobs go.

I wanted to buy a house. Dad believed that all smart seventeen year olds should (in descending order) go to university to be a psychologist, or learn a noble craft, as he called it, or be a stud and bohemian. At least have a social life. *Not* leap out of high school into two full-time jobs.

But I was simple: I wanted to buy a house. A brick house, big, on an eastern lake. To do this I shovelled gardens and pruned trees all day, then sold smokes, burritos and breath mints starting midnight. When I landed the 7-Eleven job Dad panicked and offered to pay my way to school, even my own apartment. He announced this as loud as some exasperated New York Jewish father on television. He probably came an inch from offering me 7-Eleven's wages just to come home and get a good sleep every night.

He wanted me to become a psychologist. I wasn't sure why, but I think it was because he knew absolutely nothing about it. Whenever I described one of my friends, or when we watched Jay Leno before I left for work and I snickered at some sequin-minded actress, Dad would nod his head and say again, "Yes. I think so. You should be a psychologist." And then, "Goddam it, Jimmy, you've had A's all your life."

One excuse I used went like this: Dad, you wouldn't believe the people who come into a 7-Eleven in the middle of the night. They're unbelievably *psychological*.

I suppose you're right, he'd answer, his face rigid now. He'd tell me, Sure, I suppose at your age drunks are interesting enough.

I'd be ready. Yes, I'd say. I've learned that drunks are either eagerly witty or eagerly morose. They wear their innermost urges on their sleeve.

Psychological tidbits I gave him. Even when I out-and-out fabricated the stuff, I could keep the peace and shut Dad up by making like a Margaret Mead of late night food stores.

What could you do with a father — who'd already made a pile — who wanted you to live his past for him and make that early turn he failed to make? I knew he would have been secretly thrilled if I'd experimented with strange new drugs, or went politics- gay- or religion-crazy. Ever since I could remember, he'd loved it that I was precocious. He hated that I pointed this precociousness at nothing.

How could I tell him: I just wanted to make money. As much money as you did, more, because even if you can't be happy with it, I know I will. I am not handsome, I am no artist or athlete, I have a minor personality. But I admit it: I want people to know who I am. The brick house is the first thing I want. So, money.

IT WAS AGAIN THE MIDDLE OF THE NIGHT WHEN I NEXT saw the kid. As before, he bought a Coke and drank it in front of the comic stand. As before, I watched him in the fish-eye mirror. I began to notice a strange way he had, what I came to call his "special aura" (what else do you call something invisible about a person, yet obviously there?)

For a time, I thought it was just his snottiness. He had a sarcastic bent, common enough in kids his age, but one that had its own weird feel. For instance, this second time he visited my store he bought some comics, two Scrooge McDucks. Now, I'd always loved Scrooge McDuck. That grand, unashamed lust for money. No excuses, no hint of social comment when Scrooge bulldozes his dough into great heaps, when he bathes in gold coins or rolls on dollar bills like a dog with an itchy back. Remembering, I gave the kid a wide smile as I bagged his comics and took his money.

He looked at me, cocked his head, paused, then said, "I'm buying these for my daughter."

Maybe he'd thought my smile condescending, labeling him a kid who read comic books. In any case, his wasn't the usual ten-year-old-kid sarcasm, which is about as funny and as intelligent as a yappy poodle.

A similar exchange followed a week later. I hardly noticed the kid come in because of the commotion at the counter. Two girls, a year older than me (I recognized one who had been expelled from my high school) were drunk and buying cigarettes. One, the expelled one, was blonde and good-looking in a pointy, painted way, and for some reason was giving me a hard time, thrusting the cigarette pack in my face and saying, "What would you do if I fucking walked out with these?" And again, super slowly, nodding her head with each word, "*What the fuck would you do?*"

I had no idea why she picked on me. Perhaps she'd just broken off with her boyfriend and had decided — that night, in my store — to become a man-hater. Anyway, she hated *me*. Her friend also sneered but looked less eager to rob and assault me (when I met her eyes she dropped them), and she pulled on the blonde girl's sleeve to go. The more she pulled, the more the blonde looked hot to bite my face. I admit I was getting anxious.

In the middle of my dilemma the kid walked up with his Coke. Wedging himself in front of the devilish blonde he slapped his quarters down. When he looked at me his eyes were bright, and I saw the trace of a smile.

"Well, Jim," he said. "Forget it. *Yours* doesn't like you."

The blonde stepped back to get a look at him, her rage stalled. My guess is that his squeaky voice and size is what saved him. The friend, the one who was by implication "his," looked him over, smiled, and managed an uncertain giggle. In the end the girls paid and left and all was forgotten, except the new impression I was given and which grew over the days to come — that this kid was no sarcastic poodle, but a superb ironist of life.

THERE WERE OTHER TIMES, OTHER QUIPS. LIKE THE NIGHT he bought the suntan lotion. Again, it was the middle of the night. Outside, spring had hardly shown — in fact there was a storm. You could hear the wind, and gusts would hurl sheets of rain against the windows, as though the store was a giant car I piloted through some vast wet street.

Up he came, and he laid the suntan lotion on the counter. Knowing the kid now, a little, I wondered if this wasn't a small joke, but instead of the "Nice weather we're having" you get from most people, this dry-as-toast kid was acting it out. So I was surprised when, as I smiled and nodded to acknowledge his joke, he simply pushed me the money for the lotion. I raised my eyebrows to ask if he was indeed serious, buying suntan lotion on a stormy night. He answered by sliding one white, thin arm out of his jean jacket. Bending it to parody a flex, he whispered, "You're looking at the next bronze miracle." His face stayed inscrutable throughout.

This night is fixed in my mind because — besides the storm, besides the suntan lotion — as the next bronze miracle double-palmed his way out the glass door into the night he stopped, turned to me and said, very clearly, "We have ten nights."

I ADMIT THE KID BECAME A BIT OF AN OBSESSION. THOUGH I never made a Jodie Foster out of him, like most obsessions he stayed more my fantasy than fact. I admit this too. As a result, he's now come between me and my goals. That is, my brick house.

After he bought the suntan lotion, and after five straight nights went by that I didn't once wise-ass at Leno and his feverish moron guests, Dad asked me what was wrong. By way of answering I could do nothing more precocious than grunt. How could I tell him life had gotten complicated? For the first time, I'd met a person I could not begin to figure out. Was it pride that kept me from explaining this to Dad? More likely I just didn't want to admit to myself the growing number of bafflements coming at me at once. For instance:

What did he mean, "We have ten nights"?

Why wouldn't he talk to me? Because I did try. Whenever I asked him about his jokes, his puzzles, his messages, I was treated to dark eyes filming over, the light in them — like that hint of gold hidden in the middle of a raisin — going out, and him turning back to his comic rack or out of the store altogether.

How did he know my name? Maybe I only imagined he called me Jim, but I don't think so.

More important than that, how did he read me so well? Once, when I was still nervous about fights and thieves, car tires squealed off in the darkness and such was my paranoia that I started to sweat. The kid was at his comics; two or three others shopped here and there. A minute went by but, absurdly, I was still on alert because of a sound I alone had heard or cared about. Another minute passed when up strode the kid, wiping his brow in mock grand relief. He said, "Boy, thank goodness. They're robbing another store."

And then there were his "riddles" — as good a word as any to call them. I recall what may have been the first, the Hillary Clinton one. He told it to me one of the few times he came in at dawn. There he was in front of me, out of thin air. He looked tired and bought nothing. He simply said, "What do you get when you peel Hillary Clinton?" My surprise wouldn't let me even begin to think of an answer, so I just shrugged.

"I don't know, what?"

"Pain."

That was it. He turned away, not seeing me pause then nod once in appreciation of this other-than-ten-year-old humour, if humour had anything to do with it. By the time I was into a chain of questions — *Her* pain? Common *human* pain? *Our* pain at seeing vulnerability? Pain of a non-joke? — he had left the store.

And what was I to make of this: in he walked one night, up to my counter dragging one foot behind him as though he pulled something impossibly heavy with it. He stopped and spoke with complete seriousness.

"I've been hauling the Grand Canyon behind me all day, but as soon as I go out that door it'll be like walking into a heaven."

With that he turned and began his laborious way toward the door, dragging the foot, toes pointed down to grip a canyon's edge. He didn't hurry like kids do when they're on the verge of a punchline. His posture stayed serious, his pace dreadfully slow. When he reached the door finally and exited through it he simply broke into a run across the empty parking lot and disappeared into the darkness. He didn't once crack a smile, interrupt his act, or look back to see if I watched. In the quiet of the store his pace, his discipline, was *lurid*. And, I thought, "*a*" heaven?

What was I to make of these things? In the end I came to be faced with several possibilities concerning the kid. One, the least likely, was that he was too dumb to remember how jokes went, and all his other bits of wisdom were just dumbly accidental. Two, he was a ten-year-old prodigy, a Salinger kid, one with an ear for the strange. Or, three, he was something I couldn't explain. Something more than just smart, or even regal; someone who took the word precocious into another realm entirely. And, at ten years old, an oddest teacher possible.

I suppose I didn't explain my problem to Dad because I didn't want to admit how hard psychology could get if you followed it into the area of bronze miracle kids.

I DISCOVERED SOMETIME INTO MY JOB THAT 7-ELEVEN LONEliness is a special kind of loneliness. Being alone takes on a morbid tinge when it happens in the middle of the night inside a glass box lit up with circus colours. It's an odd, empty feeling to stand there waiting for someone to come in, all the while surrounded by twinkies and ding-dongs in their bright wrappers, the gum, the pop, the neat rows of tins sitting like spectators watching the most boring sport on earth (*you* are the sport, you are the only thing *moving*), and the "produce" — about twenty sad apples and oranges and a bunch of green bananas displayed behind thick glass doors, like some exotic food in quarantine. The ceiling's noisy fluorescent glare of course adds an extra edge, and everything seems a little urgent.

But money made the lonely night worth it. I didn't even mind the constant tiredness when I stopped to think that, in a few years, after I started investing, and after a bit of luck, I could quit one of these jobs. But it was a simple contrast that got me through those nights — the contrast between 7-Eleven and a brick house on an eastern lake. I knew investment was the key. Some people I knew were bugged by the stock market, the morality of it. They seemed to think that any money made was money out of someone else's pocket. But I had no problems with that. Ever since I was a kid about the age of the bronze miracle I knew the world was more complicated than that. I knew there was no blame in money, no more than an eagle building a big, fat nest.

SOMETIMES HE DIDN'T EVEN HAVE TO SPEAK. WHAT SPOKE for him was that "special aura," which worked like this: even while he tilted back his Coke and flicked the pages of his comics, I knew he was thinking of *me*. By our third or fourth night, whenever he came into the store I felt certain he was thinking of me. Naturally it made me nervous. Though I never caught him at it, I sensed he watched me sideways through his strands of hair, and that if I did catch him at it his eyes would be as shiny as a rat's in the darkness. So a new layer of strangeness was added to the odd things he already said and did.

Even when I discovered that *everyone* in the store felt the same thing about him — that he thought only of them — I was certain it was me and me alone who concerned him. This had nothing to do with pride, or with wanting him to think of me. No — the feeling was really uncomfortable. I saw his effect on others. He made everyone within twenty feet jerk, look at him and then quickly look the other way, as if searching for that special, unstocked brand of breakfast cereal. He made fellow magazine snoopers move along into novelties and paper products. Women switched aisles, smoothed their hair and shot him glances, dark circles forming under their eyes at the sight of him. Men cleared their throats and tried to look tougher.

It did get boring at 7-Eleven around four a.m., and this did give rise to the weirdest thoughts, but I don't think I imagined much of this about the bronze miracle.

I wondered if he was charismatic on purpose.

Even Dad got caught in the kid's rays. Before I'd been long at my job Dad started his bad habit of coming in to see me on his way to work. He'd buy a coffee, give me a quarter tip, then hang around to sip and watch me. It was six-thirty, he had plenty of time. Eventually he'd get around to announcing in a loud voice, "You look *peak*ed." Only a Jewish father could choose such a word, and use such a voice. Only one morning did he say, "You look good this morning, *good*," and that was when I'd just been in the back masturbating, which was ironic as could be since I'd only lately been surfacing above my guilt in that area — which I suspect Dad planted there to begin with.

One dawn (it was our sixth night) when the bronze miracle happened to be in the store at the same time, he greeted Dad.

"*Hello*, Mr. Mayer!" shouted the kid, full of glee and with a toothy smile, a cheap take on Eddie Haskell. His face looked brand new, but like a monster rodent. I had no idea how he knew the family name.

If Dad had been suspicious or on guard, or had more wit for this sort of thing, he would have seen he was being mocked and that he was mocked with a perfect mirror of himself.

"Well!" Dad said, surprised and pleased. "*Hello* there, young man! Off to school, are we?"

The kid continued his mimicry, which now degenerated to a hint of tongue and hard breathing that looked like an eager puppy. Ridiculous as it was, the kid's copy of the spirit of Dad's exuberance was so exact it scared me. Watching him mock my poor father I found my allegiance strangely split. Also — was his act meant for my dad, or for me?

After Dad left I tried talking to him again. For all my Dad's faults we were still very close. I was a little mad.

"So what was that about?" I made a point of turning off my normal 7-Eleven smile.

"Nocturnals suck in the morning," he answered. He didn't look apologetic or even friendly as he turned and left. I decided again he was no odd teacher, just an odd pain.

PERHAPS EVERYONE SAW HIM AS A PAIN. HE HAD NO FRIENDS that I knew of. Well, maybe one: a pretty woman in her twenties, and blind. I say "maybe" because I'm not sure what I saw. I'd just arrived at work, midnight of our seventh night. The blind lady came in while the kid stood by the comics. Her last name was Betts, which I remembered because of her breasts, which were nice, and which was the kind of association I sometimes made. She'd been in the store a few times before. It sounds crude, I know, but because she was blind I could stare at her as much as I wanted. She was pretty and often smiled, and rumour had it she translated learned foreign books.

Their exchange went like this. Taps from her aluminum cane keeping her in a straight line, Ms. Betts ventured down the comic book aisle, approaching the kid. Just as she was about to pass him he grabbed her by an arm and stuck his foot in front of her. He spoke with a squeaky and nasal meanness.

"I'll trip you if you don't buy me a Coke."

When she laughed, I was of course relieved. But when, though still laughing, she said, "Get lost," and then simply hurried out of the store, it made the whole affair odd again.

Were they friends? If so, why did she leave without buying anything? Blind people don't come in to browse. Or were they strangers, and that was the kid's way of making a funny first impression? What exactly had I witnessed there? Again, as with everything the bronze miracle did, there were at least two ways to consider it.

LONG NIGHTS AT 7-ELEVEN — NIGHTS WITH FEW CUSTOMERS — can nudge a mind into unexpected shapes. And there were so many long nights that I doubted the store would last long as a franchise. I told my Dad that the locale was a good Mac's Milk, but no 7-Eleven. He smiled at this (me losing my all-night job) but the smile flickered when, probably, he had visions of me seeking a 7-Eleven elsewhere, downtown, a rougher trade.

But those long nights could throw curves at you. Especially since I started the "dozing" — a strange state I fell into when I sat for long spells on my milk crate behind the counter. This practice grew out of my attempt to learn how to sleep sitting up. Leaden tiredness clashed with my fear of actually falling asleep on the job (and getting caught) to form a thick buzzing state that in a horrible way felt more wide awake than ever. Into this state stark memories and fears would swirl and expand, sometimes, into what were maybe visions. I don't know. But if visions are what they were, then visions are not necessarily nice, and after several colourful, painful flights of fancy I decided to stop the nonsense. It was a psychology I wasn't interested in.

In any case it was during one of these "dozing" spells that the bronze miracle and I had our second-to-last meeting. It was our ninth night. It was the meeting that startled me most and the one I most remember. It had two parts.

First, a tap on the head. He must have sneaked in, leaned over the counter and rapped the top of my ripe head with a finger. The shock I suffered is hard to describe. It was the worst kind of hand-shoots-out-of-the-grave shock. As if the surprise weren't enough, something huge was added due to my already precarious state of "alert daze." His tap launched me; it injected me with forty cups of horror coffee. I couldn't move, or think, but inside I howled like a jet engine. Looking back on this experience I wonder if I'm not being over-imaginative by saying that the tap had the effect of laid-on hands, the dire jolt of prophetic words, or the grace of a king's sword to the shoulder. That is, a transplanted power. But I really can't say how clearly I'm seeing it.

The second part of our exchange was clear enough. Seconds after the tap, a piece of paper wafted down to my feet. I was rising now and turning, and I caught a glimpse of the kid retreating into the night. I picked up the paper and read:

DON'T YOU GO WIDDERSHINS TO HUMAN EVOLUTION

By the bestsellers lay a pile of pocket dictionaries. I looked for the word but it wasn't there. I pondered a moment then phoned Martin, a guy from school who was in college now, who had admired my straight-A's-without-trying (and tried to get me to join the chess club) and who likely had a fatter dictionary in his room. I was right. He yawned and grumbled about classes tomorrow but looked up my word. Probably only chess players would not find odd the burning need to know a word's meaning in the middle of the night.

He yawned through the definition. I made him read it twice before I let him hang up. Both times, when I heard the word witchcraft, my hair stood on end. "Widdershins" itself meant "going against nature, or the natural flow." In their ceremonies witches would walk counter to the sun's path in order to attract special power. Of the evil kind, I assumed.

No coffee ready, I drank two quick Cokes. I served a customer here, a customer there, but had a good four hours to wrestle with this latest of bronze miracle offerings. Before long I came upon some possibilities. One, the note was meaningless. It had nothing to do with me, and the kid was merely fooling around and showing off. Two, the note was meant for me, but I didn't understand its lesson. And, three, I did understand the note as a comment on my life. I decided on this third possibility only after hours of thinking, and the thinking took this train: If the note was for me, it looked like a kind of criticism. Well, I thought, what in my life could someone criticize? More to the point, how was I "going against nature"? How was I moving counter to evolution?

By dawn I'd found the answer. I ran against evolution because I ignored adventure, shunned ideas, refused to explore my own and the human mind. It wasn't so simple a matter as my not "going to university and studying psychology," but in the largest sense the note was hinting that Dad was right about things and I was wrong (and, in a flash of ugly paranoia caused by no sleep, I saw the bronze miracle as Dad's paid agent, and the note Dad's ingenious idea to twist my thinking his way — but, no, Dad wasn't that smart).

So that seemed to be the note's message. By dawn I was certain, so certain that my back went straight and I could bag purchases and make change ambidextrously, without looking. But what was I supposed to do? And who said the note was *good* advice? So what if some note was telling me that my vision of money and a brick house was an easy road I'd built myself, an easy road and therefore a trap? That my dreams were a cage? A gilded cage, I knew was the expression. My lord, I thought, as I stood there bagging and making change — as I sweated and trembled in defiance, but really wanted to whimper my indecision (I was so tired) — my lord, it looked like the kid, the bronze miracle, was out there in the night trying to save me from what he saw was a wasted life.

The tenth night arrived, and I stood shaking behind the counter. I was cross-eyed with fatigue and questions. The buzzing state was horrible. I had had straight A's, I was a respectable member of the workforce. Why should I listen to a ten-year-old about my future? I couldn't get him out of my mind. I felt certain that, even from a distance, he thought of me and me alone. The fact that he could walk in here at any time — but did not —

drove me crazy. He seemed to be everywhere. That he might be God hadn't occurred to me until mid-day, when I had lain wide-eyed in bed, no hope of sleep (I had failed to show at my day job for the first time ever). Though I was no believer, and though I was almost delirious when the notion rose, it did seem perfect: he was mysterious and powerful, he was wise but vague, he gave hints but never any answers. Who else but God could do that, I thought, trying to gather myself and at least tone down my shaking as I stood there in a store which — empty and silent save for the flourescent drone and machine clicks — now seemed more like a church readied for his entrance.

Our final exchange was short.

In he came, around two. A drunken businessman-type stood weaving as he flipped girlie magazine pages, and in the candy section a couple on a date giggled (they looked stoned) for too long a time over which brand of gum to buy. The kid waited for these three to leave before bringing over a Coke. (I had decided against it, but part of me wanted to have one open and ready for him on the counter, an acknowledgement of something.)

Still, I decided to be dramatic with him for a change.

"Time's up," I said, trying to sound as confident as a full partner in this ten-night riddle. But we both knew I lied, and the bronze miracle one-upped me by staring at me like he didn't have a clue what I was talking about. Unabashed, but desperate due to the finality I sensed in the air, I kept at him, trying to get my chisel in a crack.

Using the whisper of cohorts, I said, "I know exactly what your note meant."

His response was cool puzzlement.

"Did you write that note yourself?"

In answer to this he copied perfectly a puppy tilting its befuddled head. A faint light in his eyes betrayed that he was having the time of his life. No one can blame me for losing my temper.

"*You're* a fucking — " I paused, already breathless. I held my hands in front of me like I was holding his neck, and shook them. "*You* are ... You ..." I breathed through my nostrils, stared at him. Then looked up into the cigarette rack over my head, the kaleidoscope of brands. "I don't know what you are."

Now the bronze miracle smiled. A true smile, of — let me say — friends. His face muscles relaxed, had dropped any act. And what went eye to eye between us then seemed more reliable than words. He was glad, even grateful, that I couldn't think of what to call him. That I didn't have a label, or a name. It wasn't that he wanted my confusion; it was simply that he wanted me to drop my certainty. That was it: he hated certainty, he hated people being so sure.

His smile now was humble. With the warmest look I've gotten from any human before or since knowing him, the bronze miracle ended our brief friendship.

"Read about me in the news," he said, and then he was out the door.

ONCE MORE, HE LEFT ME WITH NOTHING BUT PUZZLES. It took me a week to solve the first one. During the days following our last meeting I of course scoured the daily papers for some picture or story about him. In case I'd misunderstood his instructions I even watched the late news instead of Jay Leno (and it drove Dad crazy that I wouldn't explain — but how could I?). Finally, one night I arrived at work to find the bundle of our local weekly, *The North Shore News*, and I knew he had meant not the "the news" but *The News*.

When I read the paper cover to cover and found not just one but two stories possibly about him, I almost panicked. Which one was it? Each story seemed too perfect.

The first story, on page one and continued on page two, revealed the tragic details of an eleven-year-old boy, one Ricky Cooper, who had climbed a power pole *in the middle of the night* and had gotten hung up in the lines and was badly burned about the head and hands. As tactfully as possible the article hinted that the boy's face was more or less gone. He would live but would lose the use of this hands, would require much surgery. Reading this, I sat down. A customer had to yell at me to get me to serve him.

The second story — which I almost didn't see due to my shock — began on page two and reappeared on page sixteen. Entitled "Lucky Youngster Sends Mom to Korea," the article announced that a local ten year old, Raymond Burkestone, had won a million dollars in the lottery. He'd saved money from "pop bottles and things" — which he foraged for at night? — and, being underage, had gotten a friend to buy him the ten dollar ticket, which he then gave to his mother. Mrs. Burkestone told *The News*: "'This is for you and Father,' Raymond said to me that morning, and indeed it was!" It seems the father worked most of the year in Korea on a "science project," but now with all that money Raymond and his mother could join him there. Reading the story, I got the sense Mrs. Burkestone wasn't telling all about her and her husband, but that's just my guess.

So, which one? I couldn't decide. Depending on my mood I switched back and forth. Neither name — Raymond Burkestone, Ricky Cooper — suited my bronze miracle. But I knew one of them must be him.

I have to say now that, strange as it may sound, I came to see that it doesn't matter which, because (and I know this is crazy, and really *must* be my imagination) deep down I feel that both are him, both at the same time. To me, the bronze miracle looked exactly like a combination of a kid millionaire and a boy destined to live out life with a charred face. He's both, I know he is, and I can't explain it any better than that.

IT RAINS SO MUCH HERE. BUT RAIN IS A KIND OF WILDNESS that liberates a city from itself.

Since I've taken to wandering these streets in the middle of the night I sometimes feel like I'm in some old film noir: the amplified dripping silence, the way the pavement glistens with street lights. Lonely cars slooshing their late way home, drunk and careful. Nosing out of alleys, the stern beams of cop cars on a prowl.

For a while, even when it rained, I wore nothing but a T-shirt. After catching back-to-back colds I decided I was pushing the symbolic stuff, and the emulation, a bit. Now, with my jean jacket on, instead of chilly pacing I can stand still for a long time and just sort of stare out over the glistening streets — which seems closer to the point of it all. I sometimes catch myself in this pose: just standing still, my eyelids half-closed (but my eyes awake behind them), feeling like a quiet eel swimming in one spot against a slow equatorial current. Just watching. No widdershins fish, I tread water. Without getting too psychological about it, in my street-corner pose I remind myself of the smart fish who hangs out in the middle of the aquarium, who unlike the others has quit the endless knot of nose-bumping against the glass walls, looking for some place to go.

I was surprised: there are quite a few of us out here. But we're as wary of each other as we are of anyone else.

I no longer think he's God, and in fact I feel a bit embarrassed about my imagination. I don't know what he was. But he did what Dad and school and society couldn't — he made me see myself up close, as if in a fish-eye mirror.

Quitting 7-Eleven has more or less submarined my plan to buy that lakeside house. I didn't decide not to buy it — quitting the job decided for me. You could say that doing nothing is itself a kind of decision. By standing on street corners all night I've decided not to be an astronaut, etcetera. I no longer trust people who decide to do things, who decide at eighteen, for instance, to enrol in university to become a psychologist. Such a narrow street as that shuts off every other street in the world. By doing nothing, every street lies open at my feet. Anything that's meant to happen, can.

I see clearly at night, in the rain. I watch for signs. I don't expect them to come in the guise of a boy any more. It might be an ad on a bus, it might be a bronze bird poking through the garbage of an alley, it might be a bad-mood guest on "Jay Leno." It might come from Dad, in words he doesn't know he's said.

I see that to make money, to go East, against the route of the sun, to buy a big house, is insane. In the meantime, I must do nothing. I *must* not go against the natural surge of things. Decisions — I know he'd say — are as unnatural and dangerous as witches' spells. It's so vain for a person to think he knows what's best to do in life, which is to presume he knows what life means in the first place, which is to pretend away his true underwater vision, which is our heritage and our right. People who make decisions are mentally ill. I will never be able to make my father understand that, now that he thinks *I* am.

I don't expect to seem him out here, though I can't deny it's a hope of mine. But I won't let hope obscure my view of these streets. I suspect he's left the area anyway. By left I don't mean he's gone to Korea or he's strapped to a hospital bed. By left I mean he's chosen another realm of influence. Who knows who he's operating on now? The people he chooses are the luckiest. Whether they know it or not, they are blind men at midnight finding a jewel in the wet leaves of the gutter.

I sometimes see Jhana Betts tapping along in the nighttime too. She smiles, looks a bit smug even. She knows she is more talented here than the rest of us. Maybe one night I'll sneak up and threaten to trip her. She'll laugh, say "Get lost," we'll both know, and it'll be perfect.

THE
NORTHERN COD

EYES HARD ON THE FOREIGN, charcoal hue of the Atlantic, Ruth Twirling decided she could feel its barrenness in her abdomen, its lack of fish as a negative presence, an amassed ghost of *Gadus morhua*. It was the kind of clairvoyance she as a scientist sometimes allowed herself.

The water, the rocks, the sky — a hierarchy of grey. She smiled at her exaggeration. It had been her choice to come to Newfoundland's easternmost reach, the farthest you could get from Vancouver, and she wondered at it now, why this extreme. Colleagues joking about the Pacific not being big enough for her. At her obligatory going away "do" in the Biology lounge, Murphy, a salmon man like her, had put his eyebrows up to say, "I've always suspected messianic tendencies," which Ruth took as a joke. Murphy was the closest she had to a friend in the department.

Sven had thought it was okay, her going.

She stood on the Champney's West dock, saying to herself, "Sven, Sven," feeling its curve, feeling how a name can be both alien and familiar. Hey, he'd said at the airport, have a good time out there. His body already leaning away from her, toward the car.

A minute ago a small stampede of sheep had confronted her on the lane and made her jump aside and laugh despite the sudden recognition it gave her of the real weirdness of this place. No store, no streetlights. These twenty houses, nearly windowless boxes dropped like scat on the treeless expanse of rock and into the nooks of hill bottoms. Seeing the sturdy build of the houses and feeling the steadiness of the wind on her neck came as a single sensation.

Sven, so casual. *She* still found her wildness surprising. Forty, married, flying sea to sea to save another ocean's protein. It was *professionally* eccentric in any case.

She stomped her feet loudly on the dock, instantly self-conscious. She'd been warned, but this was too cold for October. She had the new down jacket on, but otherwise cotton slacks and stupid little deck shoes. They said November wasn't much different from October and "dat's how she went 'round the calendar, b'y." This dock was strange too. Like so much here it was primitive but functional. Its slats weathered to ivory, it sloped into the water and eerily beneath, the slant the same as a wading pool, in effect a wooden beach for wooden boats, smooth for hauling and no damage to a keel. This dock was the village heart, for centuries its portal to food and peril. Ruth scanned the water and took a breath, which tried to absorb the cold salt essence of the place.

Behind her a pickup crunched gravel. She startled and turned. As it rolled by, two unshaven young men watched her, unblinking and unapologetic in their appraisal, one actually leaning across the other to do so. Ruth turned quickly away. Why were they staring, for which of the several reasons?

RUTH TWIRLING LIVED ON ACADEME'S FRINGE. GOING JOB TO job with her M.Sc. yet never into doctoral work denied her tenure, but her success with salmonid magnetic response kept her in publications, grants, lab space, grad students. At department parties she couldn't miss the envious fever some colleagues suffered at the sight of her. Generally men who hadn't published lately. And when, on borrowed equipment, she demonstrated the second immune-enhancing gene in coho, a gene fish farmers around the globe would now soon know about, a gene the existence of which some colleagues had doubted in print — once that happened it was all over. *Maclean's* magazine, two radio shows, it was trembling good fun, and her lack of a professorship was the hook upon which the story dangled and flashed. In the coffee line in the Biology lounge she faced the smiling malice. She stayed focused in the lab; biology was not a personality contest.

HER NET-SHACK LAB STOOD ON STILTS. AT HIGH TIDE THE water rose up close beneath and she imagined she could feel its cold in her foot bones. To peer out the shack's single window she had to hunch and her back had begun to hurt. If they thought she looked strange before, look at her now, with long underwear on the outside of her slacks. The shack was unheated, the long johns stretched and the pants didn't, so there you go. Maybe they wouldn't notice, everything was backwards here. For instance, both the net-shack and her cottage were waterfront, yet neither had a window on the water. The window she hunched at framed a dumpy house and its garage containing a rusty pickup on blocks. Kids played in it, and yesterday a girl and boy who couldn't have been twelve had climbed into the cab and started necking and then sank right out of sight.

HER NERVOUSNESS HAD HER ON THE EDGE OF SMILING. Tomorrow she would fertilize the eggs. Actually, tonight. At

3:17 a.m. this shack would house a rich commingling spawn. The Darwinian miracle, the gleaming trade of chromosomes, the exchange of fire for fire.

Her back to her tank and pump and hoses, feeling pleasantly the mad scientist, Ruth hunched lower at the window to see up the hill. Most every yard had its discarded nets, engine parts, rusted car. (A formula: under the quaintness of sheep lies sheep shit.) Was it like this before the fishery died, the waters still thick with *Gadus*? The clear dockside water showed its history in jetsam — bottles, batteries, braids of rust, all resting on an underwater midden of shucked scallop.

Ruth startled, dipped out of sight. It was the old crazy, five feet away, looking right in. Maybe he could still see the top of her head. The day she arrived in her rented car she'd stopped him strolling a half mile out to ask where Taylor Cottage was. He'd puzzled at the sky then nodded and began trotting off. It didn't look like he was fleeing her. No houses in sight, Ruth yelled could she please drive him but he shook his head, leading her like a rickety dog for the ten awful minutes it took. At Taylor Cottage she thanked him and there was delirium in the way he smiled, nodding.

Now right against the glass, looking in. Ruth pictured him out there with his pants down, though this was nonsense. Still, she crawled ridiculously to the corner, shaking her head at herself as she did. She should invite him in, explain her work. Was it her shyness or her assumption that he was not worth talking to? She'd never been good at people. Sven had lately been telling her to loosen up, leave off work awhile, have fun. There was something unnerving in a controlling and humourless Swede telling you to have fun.

The old man had gone. She moved to the tank, ran her hands protectively over its rim. It was a zinc-plated laundry tub, industrial size. Ben Tillmann, a colleague from St. John's, had overseen its installation and that of the pump and the hoses that ran from the shack into the water to a depth of exactly one hundred and thirty feet. The water had to be cold for conception to occur and for the zygote to divide and grow, so unlike the hot swamp humans need. This meant either refrigeration or source water. Ruth always liked to work with the source.

She flipped the toggle and the pump jumped on, its seeming eagerness a thrill. Some pieces of equipment could become pets. Its surface roiling, the water in the tank renewed itself.

THAT NIGHT — 2 A.M. ACTUALLY — SHE DROVE THE THIRTY kilometres to Trinity to call Sven. The payphone stood flourescent blue outside a tavern, Rocky's, through the doors of which she could hear the faint rasp of "Maggie May." She wondered how late Rocky's stayed open. The timing was perfect though. She had to stay up for the spawning, and it was by now nearly 10:00 in Vancouver and, no night owl, he'd be home.

DIALLING, SHE FELT THAT EDGE OF A FIRST DATE, EXUBERance pressed into its box of restraint.

This was her second call from this phone. Four days ago their talk had been brief with Sven late for a meeting. He'd sounded happy to hear her, happy with her at this distance, just as he'd been happy at the airport. She'd found herself able to return his light and shouty tone. They'd always been good at cheerful. She'd always considered this a proof of their compatibility, rather than what she heard it to be now, a lubricant to keep things smooth.

Though in a hurry that first call, he'd kept to small things.

"Cold? It's really warm here! Except there's a branch of red leaves in the maple. Funny how single branches can — "

"We have a maple tree?"

"The maple. You know, in with the cedars. The back yard."

A mathematician, Sven could be competitive with her in what he saw as her domain, what he called "nature."

"Well, the trees out here are all so small, dwarfed. Little pines."

"You're sure they're not fir?"

"I think they're pine." Though now she doubted they were.

As he chatted quickly on about life in Vancouver she pictured him at her going away party — where he'd had the myopic bravery to invite Elaine. He'd been explaining Nadeau's Theorem to an historian and had interrupted his monologue with a smile and the apology, "Sorry, I'm stumbling, I'm pretty pissed." Ruth had heard this confession before and it always surprised her. For he hadn't stumbled. He'd been lucid, precise and over-cautious. This enigma always brought from others blurts of, "Oh but you're not. Not at all." Or sideways glances, as in, Is this a subtle bragging? But an hour later, pissed he was indeed. Making a fool of himself, the bellowing laughs at nothing, cutting through his thirty years in Canada with ease, his flat and alien humour revealing to all — Ruth was sure — just how foreign he was, how impossible it was to understand him. He'd left Sweden when he was twelve, but whenever he found those raw herring at a salad buffet he'd get this look on his face. He'd ease one into his mouth and, brow knit less in appreciation than sincerity, he'd say, "These are really good." The 'good' honked with a vestige of accent, and Ruth would once again find herself seeing him as a man she'd just met and had no feelings for.

She stared at the handpainted Rocky's sign as the phone rang in their bedroom thousands of miles away. Ruth pictured Sven's long body under the quilt. The last call he'd finished with a breathless question before hanging up, "So you're calling Sunday? after dinner? is that right?" This cheerful checking up had startled her, its transparency. She could picture Sven telling Elaine that he had to go, it's Sunday, it's six, his wife was going to call from Newfoundland. Elaine smiling in sympathy. Tanned, she would be wearing white. Elaine Butt was loud and obvious, American, a psychology prof. She'd exploded through two famous faculty relationships. Once at a party Ruth had overheard her shouting in a circle of men, "I'm not a criminal, I'm a flirt!" and the men laughing with her. Ruth had first suspected Sven after she'd mocked Elaine's unlikely last name and he'd laughed in a nervous and over-eager way that suggested he'd agree with anything as long as it kept things easy for him.

The phone ringing beside their bed. Ten in Vancouver. Sven no night owl. How long did you let a phone ring before it moved from practical to hopeful?

UNDER THE STARES OF ROCKY'S BARFLIES SHE'D BOUGHT a strong coffee for the drive home and now she was jittery from it as she took the twin chrome canisters from the fridge and carried them to the bathroom where the light was better.

Placing them in the sink she gingerly unscrewed the top off the eggs. A quick look. A porridge, a grey cream of wheat, so unlike salmon. Another species, another ocean. Maybe arrogance was indeed the word. Owning these *Gadus* ova felt like larceny.

She removed the lid from the sperm and sniffed its milkiness for spoilage, to which it was prone. She loved when science allowed her to use her nose. The sperm again reminded her just enough of human that she laughingly found herself picturing a sleek, amorphous kind of cod-Sven. Then Sven not home, and what by his absence he was more or less proclaiming.

She sat, suddenly, on the toilet. Caffeine and fatigue. She put her face in her hands. There was mildew in this place; she should cover the spawn. Instead she stared off into the greying of a marriage that had evolved in ways never discussed, never decided upon. Had Sven made some kind of decision? Or had one dumb animal thing led to another?

She so loved sharing the beginning of a project with him. Not the details but the magnitude, the spirit. Once, gaining an impressive lab for a new project, she'd brought him in at night and they'd made love on a table, rattling the sterility of beakers. He'd been quiet and quick and afterwards wanted only to leave, but his minute of fierce movement had given the room a power, a force that she imagined stayed in spirit, to be used in ways she barely comprehended.

She did understand here on the toilet how she'd often used Sven in this way, to anoint her work, her projects, which were the stages of her life. And how without him her *Gadus* project felt unbegun. Shaky, unweighted, like a net-shack whose stilts shifted in the tides.

THREE-TEN A.M., SO DARK SHE HAD TO WALK WITH CARE, she carried the spawn out to the net-shack. She felt her foot press into some sheep droppings. The new moon occurred in seven minutes. No one would know this detail of her cod being conceived under the new moon. The data would read "fertilization 17 October." She was almost embarrassed herself. But some farmers still planted by it. The full moon was for results — harvests, jails full of howlers — and the new moon was for seeds

Her tub was filled with cold, new moon water, her net-shack lab lit by a single blood-coloured bulb — no one would know the witchiness she brought to her work. She opened the twin canisters, stood with them at tank-edge. Then raised her arms and tilted the streams of egg and sperm in on each other, mixing them in mid-air, her left hand female, her right hand male as they poured. She dropped the empty canisters recklessly to the floor and plunged her hands into the water. Its swirling had thickened with the gelatinous spawn, the ooze of sperm and the grain of egg, *Gadus* now *becoming* under the deep red light. She couldn't see the joining but she tried to feel it as she moved her hands slowly and rhythmically in the rank mass, ushering, prodding, hands hungry themselves.

A few tears fell into the roiling stew. She was clear-headed enough to see the drama in this and she smiled in the midst of a sob. She hated herself for wanting anything more at this moment, her hands touching all that was rich.

CHAMPNEY'S WEST TOOK ON A LIVELY AIR AS THREE MEN hammered up frames and a walkway for Ruth's styrofoam floats. When finished they'd be at anchor in the middle of the bay. Two aluminum pens, ten feet wide and fifteen deep, waited upright on the dock, covered with netting so finely meshed they could be aviaries for fruit flies.

One of the three workers was Wendel, who'd stared at her from the pickup that first day. He wasn't a bad sort, and good-looking save for a bulge to the eyes that made her suspect his thyroid. Though he was loose with quips about her work. The pens' netting he called a jellyfish magnet that would clog within a week, or be torn apart by an angry seal. (Angry at what, she wanted to ask.) Invited into her net-shack to eye the black, dot-sized zygotes in her tank, he mocked dryly, "Yass, we'll be out catchin' these beauts in no time atahll."

They'd been alive two weeks and she felt protective. Wendel studied them further, betraying hunger at seeing for the first time the hidden life of a creature he knew intimately. He looked up at her, or rather upon her, and said, supercilious as any professor, "These fry grow thirty fathoms down, my dear. They will not flourish hanging off the end of a *dock*." Actually this was pronounced, "Dese fry grows tirdy faddoms down, m'dear. Dey will nat floorish hangin aff t'end of a *dack*."

He listened to her explanation that her hypothesis rested on precisely this problem, that the reason they grew at such depth had less to do with needing pressure than with avoiding deadly ultra-violet light, and that the protective pigment spliced into a female *Gadus* two generations ago would let them grow close to the surface. That is, in fish farms.

"And where yuz gonna grow da farmers?" was all Wendel had to say about that, though he said it with a wink.

After lunch of the second day Wendel had beer on his breath, and despite her paying him by the hour he twice sat down on the job to leisurely have another. This he did smiling and looking at her in a way that invited whatever kind of confrontation she might decide upon.

She decided to surprise him.

"May I have a beer?"

His smile didn't change. "No, you may nat."

Ruth looked quickly out over the water, and then to her feet.

"Yeah, you can have one." He rose, smile unchanged. "Just jokin'. Can't refuse the boss lady, can I?" Cain't refyeas the bass lady, kin oy.

EQUIPMENT HAD TAKEN OVER HER BATHTUB. ONE EVENING she could no longer stand it and found herself at Rocky's for the coin-operated shower in the basement. Clean and refreshed, and stealing a single glance at the pay phone, a whim took her into the bar where she ordered a Johnny Walker — the aperitif habit she and Sven had developed together though she didn't recall when. She regretted the scotch as soon as she sat down, for it meant getting smoke in her hair while it was drying. Everyone here smoked.

She wasn't surprised that she knew half of the dozen people in the tavern. The bald owner of the grocery. The sullen young man who took tourists out whale watching. Away off in the corner, Wendel played pool with a fellow she knew was Boyd, the other one in the pickup that day. Pronounced Bide. The only woman besides herself worked the bar. Men's lascivious shouts told her this was Darlene. The place was windowless, with cheap wallboard. It had the spirit of a teenage boy's rec room. Mismatched chairs, brown shag, a tile square worn from dancing. Dart board so pocked and torn it was almost dry mush. A hand-routered sign beside the bar read, *AVOID HANGOVER'S STAY DRUNK.*

She knew it was loneliness that made her order a second scotch; she also knew they wouldn't befriend her. She'd long suspected what an insult she was. A fockin insult. A woman, more educated than any four of them, come to fix the fish they'd hunted to the brink of extinction, come to fix their life for them the stupid bastards.

She left the second scotch untouched. She was driving in any case. She passed Wendel on her way out and he asked, "Leavin?" to which she smiled and nodded. At the door she glanced back to see him toasting her with her scotch and downing it to the laughter of everyone in the bar.

THE EMBRYOS WERE THREE WEEKS FROM THEIR TRANSFER to the pens out in the bay and she was nervous about any number of things. Her latest faecal sample showed a rise. Not a lot, but any rise was bad. She wondered if it was due to the flock of geese new to the bay or, good god, to the addition of her own flushings? And wisps of angelhair seaweed were shooting into the tank, which announced the possibility or the hose intake becoming clogged with it. Was it her imagination that the flow had weakened? When she phoned Ben Tillmann in St. John's he sighed when she asked him to come out and help inspect the hoses, and suggested she was jumping the gun.

She knew paranoia was a creeping condition and that she must more carefully supervise her thought patterns and their vergings into the improbable. She'd been "talking" to the zygotes, for instance, and had intuited less-than-positive "answers" from them, cries for help in effect, and she knew she had to keep tabs on herself. Also, whenever the cottage furnace came on, its distant growling made her visualize a sports car rounding the corner into Champney's West, the sports car belonging to someone who was on his way to see her. The furnace had come on perhaps fifteen times and you'd think by now she would be picturing "furnace" instead of "sports car." She could smile at this. But she did decide that her sense of the village sheep not liking her was accurate.

IT WASN'T HER IMAGINATION THAT SOME OF THE ZYGOTES began to die. Not a lot but some. She knew because in death they'd pale to tan then cream before disintegrating into the flux of the tank water, into the source from which they came. She didn't know if it was the seaweed, or zinc leaching from the tank, or the aggressive fertilizer of her own stool or that of the geese. She didn't know if it was because in the wild they lived in the deeps swaddled by immense pressure. She didn't even know if it was a natural rate of zygotal loss.

She sat by the tank, staring in, watching for any healthy black zygote going pale. She lost track of time and her eyes lost focus. Once she woke with her forehead on the cold metal rim, a lock of hair trailing in the water. Another time she found herself staring into the broth dumbly mouthing her husband's name, an idiot's mantra.

SATURDAY MORNING, SHE FOUND HERSELF AT ROCKY'S early. She hadn't slept and she felt hot, grainy. She'd told herself the trip was for a shower, but once there she knew it was to call. Nine o'clock here, it was 4:30 in the morning in Vancouver. She didn't want to do this. But last night she'd been lonely and afraid, and yet very clear, and this mood had given her the strength to bring things to a head.

If he answered she planned to ask, "Is someone with you?" to get it out in the open. If he didn't answer the phone at all, well.

It was fitting, her standing in the bastard wind blowing rain under the blue shelter and into her face; fitting her using two hands to press the receiver to her ear, all appropriately pathetic because, yes, Sven wasn't there. It felt like milking something dry to let it ring, for she truly hadn't expected him to be.

SHE PACED THE COTTAGE, MADE AND DRANK AND MADE more coffee. Then paced the net-shack. She stopped at the thought that she might be disturbing them, then saw how foolish this thought was, then how it might not be foolish at all, for there were no stomping footsteps thirty fathoms down, m'dear. She peered in, let her eyes swirl with the mass, saw some tan ones and began to panic. The healthy ones were growing, they were getting bigger and she had to get them out of here, they had taken on length suggesting head and tail which would soon keep them within the mesh of the pens, little wigglers in their healthier home. She had to get them out there into the wild bay as soon as possible. There was something wrong here in the net-shack, here in the project's heart. She was breathing heavily and sank herself to the net-shack floor, dropping her head to the rough wood planks that had suffered hard boots for a hundred years. The electric pump with its friendly song had become a part of her, and she had the waking nightmare that if it suddenly shut off, her neck would flip and break and she would die.

MORE NAMELESS DAYS OF ROIL AND PACING AND VOICES that no longer sounded like hers. She had lost her watch somewhere and didn't know the time but it looked like the light was falling. Somehow she had decided to drive back to Rocky's to call Sven and have a basic chat about their marriage. But when she arrived she walked past the pay phone without looking at it. She walked in, said hi to Wendel and his buddy Boyd, then up to the bar to ask Darlene for a beer.

She was soon at a table with a bunch of people. Rocky came over and introduced himself. He was witty and a charmer, and he asked if she was surviving Champney's West, calling it "the sheep shit capital of Newfoundland," which, even as she laughed, made her go inward to try recalling if rainfall had marked a rise in faccal count, for this would point to the sheep.

It wasn't unlike sitting back watching a big family, everyone knowing each other utterly, arguing and laughing over details of lives about which she had no clue, family members coming and going, getting up to play pool or head home for a bite, then back for another pint. Rocky brought her over a microwaved hamburger on the house after she slurred. Others prodded her, nudging the plate closer till it touched her elbow, offering opinions on her being pale and thin and that she should eat. They were such nice people and so free to say whatever they were thinking about, like children. Though once when she smiled almost wickedly at Rocky — she could be as flirty-girty as anyone when she tried — he gave her a troubled look that she couldn't read, maybe it meant he had a wife, so she shrugged and laughed and ignored him.

So the tavern wasn't that bad. It had crazy-colours and was only well lived-in. The smell of old beer didn't bother her now, maybe because she was drinking it. Black Horse, a beer brewed in Newfoundland. You did get used to things. Getting used to Rocky's didn't mean lowering her standards, it meant her noticing details of worth, of qualities appropriate to habitat. She learned that Rocky's held the church bingo, and dances for the whole region, dances attended by the most respectable of grandmothers.

Even Sven is happy I am here. She laughed saying this, mostly because people tilted their heads at her in question like puppies. She had almost gotten over her surprise about Sven. Surprise-surprise. Not that he was having an affair, but that she didn't care. On the floor of the net-shack she had had a blunt conversation and had arisen from it shaking her head at the past ten years and smiling wryly at them.

"Watcha smilin at there, eh?" For an hour now Wendel had been buddy-buddy at her shoulder in the corniest high school way.

"Cad," she told him.

"Cod? Fish?"

"Yays. Feesh." She really must try to stop mocking the way they spoke.

IT BEGAN WITH WENDEL BUYING HER THE BOURBON. BOYD stomped back in from supper and bought her another. Boyd, Bide, was friendly, a shy one, a boy. He and Wendel had way back taken a trip to Mardi Gras in New Orleans and loved someone new to tell it to, how they'd survived the women and bars and fights down there and were alive and back home here today to tell Ruth about it and buy her these bourbons, they knew good bourbon and this was good bourbon an dear may I touch your arm like this. Tooch yer airm lake dis.

"She's died, boy, and she ain't comin back." She's dyed, bye.

"Who ain't comin back?" Ruth smiling at her words.

"The fockin fishery! Jaysus, ya bin listenin?"

They were like little boys, friendly under the tough pride, and she had fun playing pool with them, letting them take turns bending over her back to help her aim, and once Wendel followed her into the ladies' bathroom, and when Rocky gave him hell Wendel shouted at him, Fock aff, ya ain't me faather. It was a lot of bourbon, a swirling in the stomach and in the head, and then her elbow hit the wall hard and she had to walk outside. After shouting down Rocky's angry offer to drive her, Wendel and Boyd drove her themselves.

Boyd drove while she played with Wendel's knee. He played with hers back and she rested her smiling head on his shoulder which made him go quiet like it does, like early love. She may have slept for now she was being half-carried laughing into her cottage, Wendel cursing the sheep shit as the three of them stumbled along. She pointed and yelled, No! There! There! at her net-shack and they cursed some more but changed course and took her in.

Boyd was bewildered but screwed in the red bulb like she asked. This request and the colour seemed to spook them. In the witchy light they whispered and joked and passed a flask and she could see their Mardi Gras bravado come out. Boyd stepped out then so it was kisses with Wendel, kisses easy and cheerful and at one point he yelled through the net-shack wall to his buddy, "Bide! So will she be firin me now or givin me a raise?" His clothing smelled strongly of oil and his skin was fish-shiny with sweat. He turned to her for more and she went limp for it, indifferent to her body.

"Get ready," she whispered. He said, "Ooo I's ready dear," but she hadn't been talking to him. She laughed at the ripping of her cotton pants and hearing this Wendel laughed back, sur-prised, his laugh nervous and husky, thinking he was getting away with something. In the blood of the light she could see Boyd hunched and watching in through the little window. With one hand Ruth held firm to the side of the tank, her fingers sub-merged so she could be with them through this, and she would not let go and be taken to the floor. Wendel cursed then pressed her up against the net-shack wall, through which she could feel the water of the Atlantic, its vast barrenness and its waiting.

MOUNT APPETITE

DEC 22ND

What were your instructions? "Write your version down and send it to me"? I'm grateful for this. I'm not good face-to-face and today was a pressurized day. Sorry for raising my voice, et cetera. Here I can craft my thoughts before blurting. Though I bet pushing the "send" button will feel like a blurt.

You also said, "Be honest with yourself and with me." You said it as a challenge but I heard it as an assessment. Well, alright. Being honest as possible I'll start by saying that I find you rude. Sure, you were in a hurry, as doctors seem to be. True, I was on my way out the door and, true, I was yelling. But "write your version down and send it to me" is insulting. It says my version is a *version*.

And my version of what? The events of that night? Simple: people came and dragged my daughter away. Or do you mean the events leading up to that night? Fine, how far back should I go? Felice is twelve. Or are you asking how I came to "administer controlled substances to a minor in my care?" That is no less complicated.

Plus I resent your implication that if I don't follow through with this I might not have your help in the investigation and all the other bureaucratic *shit*. Is honesty even possible here? Isn't it obvious that someone like me would say *anything* to get my daughter back?

I'm out on my deck, it's three in the morning, very crisp and the sky offers grapey clusters of stars. My laptop battery light is blinking at me because it's never felt this cold. But I want to tell you how helpless I feel, how I feel surrounded by galaxies of insane pettiness. Each galaxy (read: government ministry) is spinning in on itself with its mad, mad, black hole in the middle, sucking in all common sense, and decency, and light. A black hole is the absence of a brain and, even more, a heart. The word "ministry" smacks of horror. It harkens back to when government was religion, a churchy time when "ministry" meant kindness. That it flipped to its soul-sucking opposite is — well, Orwell predicted it, didn't he?

Having said all this I do feel a bit lighter. I *will* try to be as honest as possible. I want nothing except to help Felice.

DEC 23RD

Nothing you will hear from me is completely true, even this sentence. That's a good one, isn't it? Or: Everything you hear is only partly true, except for this sentence. These are some little koans I've been playing with in trying to tell you my "version."

I trust you got the first email. I do know I can't write everything down in one sitting. I get emotional, and tired, and my mind breaks into voices shooting off on *their* own "version." Last night I jumped up from this chair, voices coming off me like Medusa's snakes, and I had to leave for a good fast walk.

I'll go to the heart of the problem: they think Felice has been damaged by my behaviour, while in truth it's her behaviour that made me self-medicate in the first place.

Please — I'm not blaming her. I'm saying it's no different than when any father comes home from work, gets stressed by his child, then gulps a scotch. In fact I did use beer in this way some years back, but one beer led to six and I was a less-than-attentive dad. My switch to marijuana was a responsible act on my part. And if you can help them see the truth of this —

But do *you* believe it's true? Who's the better father, the slurring lout on the couch watching breasty sitcoms, or the dad who is focused, gets involved, in fact gets fascinated with her math homework, cooks fantastic meals, can drive her to her volleyball games, remains sensitive, even overly sensitive to her condition and her attacks?

I think it's her condition that we're both interested in. It's what I most want to talk about. I've been wondering about how to do that, exactly. You're the professional. I've merely lived with her every day of her life. (You understand my sarcasm.)

I don't care what you think about me, but if you believe me on just three points I will be grateful. I can't let you agree with them that I am "addicted to marijuana," which I am not. Or that I "grow marijuana with intent to traffic," which I do not. (The second newspaper story used the term "grow-op," which is absurd.) Or that I "contributed to the delinquency of a minor by administering controlled substances," also untrue.

The three points I need you to agree with:

1. I self-medicate because of her but it's a responsible decision, without which I would have gone down the drain and taken her with me.
2. I've grown marijuana solely for medicinal use and sell it only to free up more time to spend with her.
3. My giving her marijuana in a deliberate and measured way is also a responsible act.

DEC 23RD — LATE EVENING

Felice is extremely bright. I do get tricked into thinking that someone so bright should be able to see her way out of a mental illness, but we know it isn't that simple. History's brilliant lunatics all say so.

She is bright and always has been and I'm not just a proud father saying this. Straight A's. Uses logic like a lawyer. She can focus. (Focus too much? Is this part of the problem?) A year or two ago when she was ten or eleven, a test said she read at the university level. Felice was proud, understandably. When she took this as reason to demand from me some freedoms enjoyed by women of university age, I put my foot down. One question, "Why can't I stay out late?" made me sad, and I stumbled with my words. If you haven't gathered yet, she has no friends and no *opportunities* to stay out late. I forget what I said exactly but I twisted things around to letting her watch TV on weekend nights, till ten, if she censored herself in terms of sex and violence. In this regard I'd had an experience with Felice a few weeks earlier. We'd rented *Mighty Aphrodite* and were watching it unaware that Woody Allen's character would be offered countless blowjobs and fucks (in those words) by his love interest, Moira Sorvino (sp?). Neither Felice nor I said a word, it was all edgy and Oedipal. Most of all I realized that she knew these words.

One of the side effects of marijuana — the worst, I think — is the tendency to lose your train of thought, and I apologize for having done it. I had to reread to get back to my main point, that Felice is extremely bright and always has been.

My main point was *actually* to say that not only has she always been bright, she has also always been sick. I recall Rose having the hardest time getting her to breastfeed, even when Felice was very, very hungry. A month old, with a milky nipple nudging her lips, Felice would thrash, wild-eyed, *unable to decide what to do.* I also remember her tantrums at age two — in most ways they resemble what still happens now. The frustration, the paralysis, the way it spikes in loud display — which you say you've seen, Doctor.

I'm tired and have to sleep but the real point I want to make is that her condition was in no way a response to Rose dying. I know others don't share this view. Here's a simple proof: Felice was this way when she was two and her mother was alive. When she was three and her mother was gone, she was still this way.

As she is now, lying somewhere asleep, twelve. I hate that she's not upstairs. This time of night, she's always been upstairs, asleep. I love it when she's asleep.

Sadness is a physical thing, don't you think? You feel it deeper than your bones. At night you lie in it. In the morning it wakes you up. I can see how dwelling in sadness — *dwelling* is the perfect word, sadness your home — could lead to sickness, and death. I can see myself lying exposed on the slopes of the mountain, dying.

I can't stand that Felice has been taken from me. I know I shouldn't say anything like this but the thought of Felice somewhere, awake and afraid, makes me want to hurt the people who took her.

Please, that was no threat, but listen: Unthinking functionaries anticipate a beer after work, but first their day's final duty: tearing an unbalanced girl from her father and inducing such pain that it could conceivably make one of us die.

DEC 24TH

This is becoming more than a letter but there is so much to say — if I'm going to earn your trust and your help. Your secretary made clear to me your reactions to my previous email and I apologize. As I explained to her, I intended nothing remotely threatening. "One of us dying" referred to Felice and me, and to sadness, and if I'm guilty of anything it might be over-statement, though I'd argue that as well.

Sadness. Last night I was reminded how bad Felice can be in restaurants, what a menu can do to her. It did more than just remind me — I felt it in the pit of my stomach. It made me miss her, swelling up so hot that I almost cried. But I was with company.

You know how some people flirt with eccentricity? That's Tim and Patricia Woods, who took me to the restaurant "to help me bear my burden," as they put it. They're Christian, not too bad with it but still you can see how it's at the core of what they do, like befriending me and Felice in the first place. I sense missionary zeal. But they are very much into not judging.

In any case I saw how they like minor-league oddity. We were stopped at a light and Tim haw-hawed at the car in front of us: it had a Honda trunk logo (that Hercules H), a BMW logo on one side and a FORD logo on the other. You couldn't tell what make it was — at least I couldn't. Tim haw-hawed again, declaring it a Toyota. At the restaurant they surprised me further when they claimed their reservations under the name "Kennedy" and Patricia explained with a wicked smile that they did this every week — ate out and made reservations under the name of a political figure. They'd been Mr and Mrs Bush, and before that Gore, and they were working backwards. I chuckled my appreciation, though they weren't good with Boston accents or very clever with this game in general.

Point is, once upon a time I practised oddity myself, and to tell the truth even got a bit competitive with it. That was before Felice. A child like her can pop one's bubbles, can chain one's romp. I recall how once in a Japanese restaurant with Rose I stole a painting off the wall. Hanging in the hallway to the bathrooms, it was of an intimate circle of young sumo wrestlers-in-training and it was wonderful. I measured its width against my shoulders, took it down and shoved it up my back, under my sports coat. Very broad-backed, I side-shuffled into the restaurant proper, and sat. To Rose's horror, I fully intended to steal it. When I was accosted at the cash (Rose going silent), I went on the offensive, loudly telling the cashier, and then the owner, that they had no right to this wonderful picture if they were going to hide it in a bathroom hallway. I'm not sure they understood my English, let alone my logic. I got louder, walked the picture to a bare patch of wall over the bar, held it up with my hands and shouted that I would not leave unless they promised me they would have this excellent picture hanging on this spot by opening time tomorrow. The two men looked at each other and with a toss of the head the owner told me, I think, to get lost. In the car Rose wouldn't speak to me but an hour later she was laughing.

My point being: Felice wasn't born yet. She snuffed play. Or, another way of seeing it, she became oddity enough.

In any case dinner with Tim and Patricia had its moments but I was reminded, via my sad stomach, of Felice's difficulty with menus. In a way, her hell-dance with menus sums up her main symptoms. A restaurant goes like this:

Dinner out has been her suggestion. We make appropriate jokes about tolerating Dad's cooking for too long. We sit happily until we consult our menus. I scan mine, not really reading because I am scared shitless. I hum a tune or mumble about nice smells coming from the kitchen. Half the time, Felice will close her menu and say, "I'll have chicken strips." Or, "I feel like lasagna." This always seems a miracle to me, this reprieve. I can joke now, feel her arm and say, "You feel nothing like lasagna." In other words, sometimes we can be normal.

But half the time I get the dread sense she is taking too long, and inevitably I hear, "I don't know what to get." Or an equally hellish, "I don't know what's good." Or the utterly accurate, "I can't decide." Or the most painful, for me, "What should I get?" Sometimes it's even a quavering singsong, "Let's see." It seems whenever she says one of these it's with knowledge of where this is going — yet she can't help herself, even so early on in the tantrum, which is what I'll call it.

I try to nip it in the bud:

"Have the chicken strips. I hear they're fantastic here."

"But what if the lasagna's really good too?"

"No. Chicken strips is their specialty."

"But what if I don't like them?"

"Then you can have my dinner. I'll order lasagna and we'll trade." Or, "Sometimes that happens in life. It can be fun. We can complain about the food together." Or, "If you don't like it we'll order something else until you do." Or, "Don't be such a spoiled North American. In Ethiopia they'd beg to lick your plate." Or I'll flee to the bathroom, hoping I'm part of the problem ("take away the audience" being tip number one for tantrums). I've tried it all.

By now she's staring, stricken, into the middle distance. As if the middle distance is staring back, she'll kick a foot, even snarl. I keep trying: promises, threats, musical moans of sympathy. But now she's paralyzed. Now she's gasping. Now she's flailing. Now I'm dragging her out, Felice struggling against me because — *what the hell* — she can't bear to leave because that too is a kind of decision.

When she's out of control, the look in her eyes is of someone hanging by their nails from the edge of the mountain. Have you seen her this way? Have you witnessed her power? The shrieking? Capillaries bursting in her face? It's amazing, isn't it. It's taught me a lot.

Doctor, she's just like us. We all want the best, except we give in sooner. Doctor, *we don't care as much*. Tantrum or not, painful or not, Felice is showing us how we have given up, how long ago we settled for second best.

She's suffering for all of us, is what I think.

DEC 26TH

Look, I don't know what to do. I'm settling in again to write. I should say something about what this is doing to me. Can you imagine what it's like to sit and write these things? Knowing that the words I put here might, or might not, get me my daughter back? Do you understand that, between the words, I sometimes hyperventilate? Shouldn't I tell you this?

(I'll be *dangerously* honest with you and admit I've just had a smoke and my logic might get energetic, especially since this stuff is stronger than my homebrew.)

Shouldn't I tell you that I feel pressured to be *attractive* to you? I'm trying to seduce you. How's that for honesty? I want you to think I'm decent, smart, honest, steady, responsible, when *all I want is for you to help me get my Felice back here.*

She's not unhappy here. She's sick, and I sedate her, but no more than I sedate myself, *and she's not unhappy here.*

Describing Felice in restaurants reminded me of another time in a restaurant with someone who reminded me of Felice but in unexpected ways. He's an author, you see, pretty much a famous one, American. How we came to be together is a long story. Simply, I had enticed him with entertaining fan letters, and when he was in town he called me. He ended up not liking me much I think, because my letters were more entertaining than I was in the flesh — I was over-stoned and stiff and timid. But let me say that, though he struck one as brilliant, his earthiness shoved his brilliance way off against the wall. He was so earthy, so helplessly yearning, that watching him was like watching a fifty-pound tongue, sewn to a fifty-pound eyeball, sewn to a fifty-pound stiff penis, sewn to a fifty-pound raw heart. He was a gourmet, and since he relished good tastes with his master tongue, in a rage he flung the wine list across the restaurant because it had no wine of a certain region in France, which he claimed was the only wine that went with what we were eating, a Provençal chowder. The thing that struck me was, like my Felice, his little tantrum was somehow on behalf of everyone.

I suggest a deal. Let's put it all on the table. Here: you go to wherever she is, walk in on her, and see if she's happy. If she's happy you're doing better than me, so keep her, keep going. If she's unhappy, send her home because you're doing no better than me and probably worse.

And: I love her. You people don't, and she knew that in the

first two seconds. I really should tell you someday what Felice has taught me about Mount Appetite.

Do you actually want honesty? You did challenge me. So do you want to know what I *want*? Are you capable of telling me what *you* want? Why is the onus on me?

So, hey, let's get to know each other. Isn't it funny how we — I mean the universal we but that's still you and me isn't it? — don't talk about the thing we crave most of all? I'm talking about that thing we talk *around*, that thing in the background when we nudge-nudge wink-wink, when we advertise cars or underwear or anything at all, that thing your Freud said runs the whole enchilada. It's the mountain's main deity but we only circumambulate and dare not speak its name. Isn't it funny that guys — guys like you and me — will get into shoelace arcanery of the New York Yankees, or what colour fly catches what spring trout, or the finest print on mutual funds, but nobody — picture all these buddies sitting in a big room with us, Doctor — nobody in the room has a clue what anyone else thinks about the very best thing. Not a clue. What sounds each other makes having one, what brings one on quickest for you or for me, who likes to delay a bit. You understand my point? Wine experts go on about after-nose and fruit and length. Why don't we, all of us being experts at our own orgasms after all, have coffee-break conversations about what's way more important to us than wine?

I'll start. In the name of Mount Appetite I'm going to tell all you guys all about my favourite thing. I am forty-two years old and, having just seconds ago figured out my computer's calculator, I can tell you that I've had between five and seven thousand. Because my wife died ten years ago and I don't get out much, way more than half I've enjoyed by myself. How were they? you ask. Well alright, I'll tell you: one out of ten was exceptional. Maybe "exquisite," or maybe even "heavenly" applies here, these words used accurately by me for probably the first time. At the other end of the scale, one out of ten is so dull I might as well not have had it at all. I don't know how crude you are, Doctor, or if scatology was part of your curriculum, but maybe you've heard the expression, A good shit's better than a bad fuck. I consider this to be very much a medical observation since it describes not just the quantity but the quality of nerves firing, a kind of elite rather than steerage synapse. And those bottom ten-percenters — don't you agree that they have the soul of unbuttered potato? Since you ask: if I could attach a colour to orgasm it would be orange. A taste, sweet 'n' sour. Sometimes in the middle of one I'll crank my head hard left, I don't know why, just feels right. Sometimes I feel one throb like candy in my ankles. They say you lose consciousness during the peak second, but I've stayed with it and I disagree. It's a thoughtless state but clear-eyed as sky. I submit that it's a doorway. A sneeze is similar, maybe identical. I'll coin this: a good sneeze is better 'n a bad fuck too. And I submit that someone who took this up religiously could, after some years of study, shoot right out of themselves with an orgasm or a hearty sneeze. That's my suspicion. Where they'd go is anybody's guess.

I had a point, and I believe it's that I have no idea if Felice has ever had an orgasm. It's something I'll never ask her. Maybe Rose could've. This might be my one failure as a father.

I submit in all seriousness that it might help Felice an awful lot if she masturbated an awful lot. Why shouldn't I want my daughter to enjoy the best in life?

At least it would take the edge off. With Felice, that's what we're talking about, isn't it? That edge? Doctor? You psychology types ever consider orgasm-as-therapy, or is that simply too weird for you? Or too close-to-home? Your first-year anatomy exam should have been a gargantuan circle-jerk, hundreds of you, pencils clattering to the floor, profs urging you on, the last to cum getting kicked out and forced into law. Yoo-hoo, Doctor? Ah, ah, *ah chooooo*.

DEC 27TH

I apologize for last night. Honesty wouldn't let me not send it. Sometimes with pot I climb — fall? — to the suicidal bravery of the assassin. I hope you were at least entertained.

I want to remind you that, all her life, Felice has been on the cusp of institutionalization. Medication has gotten her through school. No, not through school but through *teachers*. It's not the work that's been hard for her, it's certain teachers. There are teachers who give clear instructions and teachers who don't. Felice needs black and white. I think it is this fundamental need that keeps her from having friends. Friends are muddy, swirly, sticky, sandpapery, vague. For Felice about as fun as a nonstop traffic accident.

I remember the first time I saw an authority figure fail her. Felice was maybe three. We'd gone to the library for story time. The librarian was pointing in a book and asking children what certain animals were, and Felice corrected her when she'd agreed with a child that that was a camel. Felice couldn't pronounce her Rs yet but "It's a *dwomedawy*" came out with calm confidence. All would've been well had the librarian acknowledged her own error and continued. It would have been okay too if she had firmly disagreed with Felice and continued. The librarian's reaction — uncertainty, self-doubt, irritation — left things hanging and unclear and instantly Felice went stiff.

What's fantastic is that her outrage isn't even on her own behalf. If a teacher is wrong it means that all the students in the room are made wrong too. Felice wants clarity for all. *Needs* it for all. One of her past teachers told me that a misspelled word on the blackboard was the worst trigger. I can just see Felice sitting there shaking, that uncorrected error hanging over them like a demon of chaos and no one doing anything about it.

If Felice even suspects a teacher of being wrong she will start to shake. And sweat. And, of late, stink. Don't waffle when you talk with her, Doctor. Especially don't contradict yourself. What happens isn't pretty.

Just a month ago we suffered one of her worst eruptions in years because Mrs Moffat, her teacher, hadn't been clear. Working on study questions for a history test the next day, Felice got stuck on, "Who first settled Canada?" She didn't know if the right answer was the French or the Vikings, who hadn't stayed all that long. How long, she asked me, do you have to stay before you can use the word "settled"? I could feel the whole room going rigid so I crept to the kitchen to start water for some of her special tea. In the time it took me to plug in the kettle and set out two cups, because I was damn well going to have some too, she had begun to tremble, and stink. It's new since her bloom of puberty, but it is the smell of animal rage. I submit that while "danger" has gotten more complex, our bodies' response to it has not.

Observing her conundrums for years, I think I know what the initial emotion is. I think we all do. It's "that feeling of injus-

tice." I've parsed it further. It's a joining of anger and fear —
fear of a disjointed universe, anger that it continues. It hits your
centre, which goes hollow. The cold sweat of frustration. Unless
you shake it, it builds. If you're Felice, it gets monstrous.

Thing is, you can't tell her the truth, which in this case was,
"Well, it depends what Mrs Moffat means by 'settled.'" Nor could
I, reformed student of the Christopher Columbus era of educa-
tion, tell the even bigger truth, that the first settlers were the
families who crossed the land bridge at Alaska, populated the
continent, and mistakenly came to be called Indians. I don't think
that's what Mrs Moffat meant by "settled" either, unless it was a
trick question to snag any remaining Eurocentric Grade Sevens.

I couldn't help Felice with these uncertainties. She doesn't
let me call her teachers on the phone. As her tantrum rose, of
course nothing came of my final, shouted, "The answer is the
Natives! The *Natives* settled here first — that is the only fucking *possible* truth, because they *did*!" In the end I got her into
the rec room and let her destroy an old pillow and wooden chair
I'd bought at a yard sale for this purpose.

Let me make my claim: an understanding father has kept
her out of institutions.

DEC 28TH

Apparently there's no name for what she has. Maybe you have
one. You head-doctors have contrary takes — versions — of
everything, yet you're all so sure of yourselves. Even of your
uncertainty. When you announce "We don't know what it is,"
you do so with formidable certainty. But this isn't about you.

Obsessive-compulsive. Autistic. Even schizophrenic. Often

with qualifiers: "mild form of" or "intermittent" or "transient-acute." Once in a mall a middle-aged woman called Felice a "big baby" when Felice couldn't decide what colour her first halter top should be. "Big baby" is, I think, the most accurate. Another good word is "perfectionist." (I've just had a smoke, Doctor, but is it my private fantasy that babies are the ultimate perfectionists? I mean, who else but a perfectionist would scream at a bubble stuck in their throat?)

Don't tell Felice this, but I find her pain completely typical. That is to say, in her pain I see mine and everybody else's when we can't make up our minds or don't get our way. We just don't feel our pain so strongly. But we do feel it. We always feel it. We are constantly unsatisfied. It's the human condition, of course. We're adept at staying pretty numb to it. Felice isn't. We grew thick skin and she didn't. When she freaks out she has no skin at all. She is a skinless, red, wet, throbbing heart. Just like we feel our shirts on our shoulders, she can feel air currents on her hot wet heart When the moth-of-doubt flies too close to her skinless heart she screams and screams and screams.

Did you know this about her, Doctor? Meet Felice.

They took her away because I gave her marijuana tea to sip, which had the effect of making her curious about moths, so to speak, instead of afraid of them. The first few times I gave it to her she giggled. Is there anything remotely wrong with a giggle? The same people who disapprove of this tea and took her from me had, in the past, given her various chemicals, most of which made her care about nothing, a few of which made her wonder who she was, and one of which made her drool.

Forgive me my anger, but I really do suffer "that feeling of

injustice" when I think of the "experts"— medical, legal, social
— crawling all over this case, sliding in probes when they see
a hole, but seeing nothing of the larger picture.

Could somebody please ask the expert? Could somebody
please talk to me?

Another thing: apparently we're all going to die and we have
only so much time. Can you tell me what any of us are *supposed*
to do under these conditions? Am I reacting any worse than the
rest of humanity to this news? Is Felice?

DEC 29TH

At first I hated the Leaches for ratting on us. But how can I
blame them? A twelve-year-old girl, wandering around their
cabin, irritable, scratching at counter-tops, mumbling, "I need
my cannabis." I think she casually asked them, as if it were crack-
ers and cheese she were after, "Do you have any cannabis?" It's
almost a little funny.

It sure ruined Christmas, which has come and gone. (And
I hope Felice is enjoying the Discman and T-shirts you so kindly
forwarded to her. Irony intended.)

It was the fifth or sixth time we'd gone to the Leaches' cabin
to hunt our Christmas tree. It's become a tradition. The Leaches
own a hundred acres of bush and invite a few families every
year to bring a saw and drag out a tree. It's just an hour from
town and it's good wholesome fun — thermoses of hot choco-
late, mince pies, barking dogs, snowball fights if there's snow.
Apple-red cheeks on the children, even Felice. The childless
Leaches sit on their couch smiling. They are both squat and
round-faced, more like sibling gnomes, and from the way they

sit so benevolently amid the chaos it's clear how much they enjoy it too. So I'm sad for them. I suppose in their straitlaced way they thought they were doing the right thing.

This time Felice stayed behind in the cabin for the actual tree hunt because last year the choice-of-tree set off a biggie. So this year we said nothing — I simply went out the door and she simply didn't follow. (Again, even acknowledging the problem can bring it on. I know she harbours romantic notions about Christmas. Settling on "the right tree for me and Dad" must be torture.) Wisely she extracted herself. She knew she could be happy with the tree I chose. She knew she could see it as the right one, if choice weren't involved. She's making some progress, she's coming to know herself.

But staying behind forced her to admit to a problem. It had seeded and begun to grow in her. She knew that cannabis might help distract her — or it.

What she didn't know was that 'cannabis' is marijuana. I'd never told her. When she asked what the tea was or what the cookies had in them — she knew they had *something* in them — I said 'cannabis.' I could have made up a name, but there you go.

Let me say two things about this: One, Felice herself was asking for cannabis, trying to repel some anguish — doesn't this open up the possibility that it might be good medicine for her? Two, the Leaches saying "she looked like she was in withdrawal" is nonsense and you know it. Even if she was "addicted," and "in withdrawal," marijuana doesn't act this way. No, she was agitated, on the fringes of an attack. If someone would only ask me, I could describe perfectly how she was moving, what noises she made, et cetera, because I have seen it, years and years of it.

DEC 30TH

I should have used the mountain, should have watched from my aerie. I should have fought from the very start. I've been kicking myself.

When they came to get her (a few days after the cops had come to serve me papers and rip the plants out of my downstairs study, which itself came a few days after our tree hunt at the Leaches), Felice and I were enjoying a perfectly corny domestic scene. My dishes, and her homework, were done. We were about to watch some TV, and I was ready to pretend I had to watch the hockey game in case Felice couldn't decide on a program. We were halfway through our cup of special tea (I have other sources) when they came.

It was two men and a woman, maybe you know them. The woman, a lawyer, was in charge. She was pretty, I've been long alone, she had a nice smile — the scenario could've been out of the TV show Felice and I never did get to watch. She smiled and looked me in the eye and said, "We'll get this sorted out." The other two functionaries weren't smiling but also looked me in the eye while nodding agreement with her. "Getting this sorted out" referred to my sudden apparent custody problem. She had a sheaf of legal papers which she smiled me through, explaining like a conspirator that these two fellows would take Felice whether I signed or not, and that my cooperation would help her "get this sorted out."

Only later did I understand that she would have said anything to deflect a father's rage and grease their legal kidnapping. One man had Felice softly at the shoulder, a hold at once friendly yet potentially forceful. I see that now. They were all sugar and butter with us. It might have been the tea, which because I'd had to buy it was stronger than we were used to, but they made me feel — and I think Felice felt this too — that our lives were now under control, we were being managed by people who knew how to take care of us. Yes, I suspect this was Felice's feeling as she was ushered along by her smiling mentors and placed in a car much newer and better-smelling than her father's. Felice's life has been chaotic and these people simply seemed so knowing. *Precisely* what would seduce Felice, but I shouldn't have been tricked.

Why didn't I gauge their appetite? I could have snapped out of my dozy hope and seen in their eyes the lack of passion in what they were doing. "Sorting this out" meant, to them, getting a girl out of the house and into the car. They were doing their job and then going for coffee. I don't and can't blame them: their job had absolutely nothing to do with "sorting out" me and Felice. I should have seen that. They were almost bored. They were punting around the mountain's middle slopes. I could have seen this in their eyes through the peephole in my front door. I should never have opened it.

Passion doesn't lie because it can't. You can see this not just in the eyes but in the breathing, in the shoulders, the crook of the neck, how the hand betrays its anticipation. You can see where they are on the mountain and see their power, or lack of it. Felice taught me this, and I should be using it more.

I should have taken Felice and run, right? Am I equally right in saying that I shouldn't be telling you that? What you all want from me is restraint, I know that. *Restraint.* What a wild word. It *proves* power. Anthony Hopkins, perfect butler. Moving not a muscle.

I look forward to seeing you tomorrow.

DEC 31ST

I was grateful for this morning's opportunity to meet with you, but now I'm scared.

If I understood you right it's no longer just the legal matter of me giving dope to my daughter, it's become a question of my "fitness as a parent." "Stability" was a word you used. "Role model." "Safe environment." These burned me to hear them. I learned you are not on my side. My mistake: I saw subtle art on your walls and the Birkenstocks on your feet and presumed your sympathy. I'm scared and I'm mad. I'm *mad*.

A "grow-op"? Bullshit. My setup is — was — modest and I never let Felice see it. It was downstairs, always locked, and we called it my study. It's a complete surprise to me that she says she knew about it. She did *not* help water or fertilize, and I have no idea why she would say she did. She wouldn't lie, but I demand to know how these questions were worded.

That I sold some on the side says nothing. No, it says lots. me selling pot lets me be a full-time father. I greet her when she comes home from school. I'm with her when she can't suffer school. I cook wonderful meals. I'm always there for her.

And *violence*? Let me tell you, I've not been ignorant of an attitude about single-parent fathers. It doesn't take long antennae to get the message. It can make you paranoid, Bub. I'm not talking suspicion of incompetence. That's a given. I'm talking suspicion of — I don't even have to say, do I? I understand where it comes from. Males of many species have a shitty track record. Daddy lions, alligators, wolves, et cetera, kill their own. Dogs howl for and hump their daughters when they're ripe. Baboons — here we're getting close to human, right? — do either one or the other.

But most human dads don't. Nor do they forgive those who do. Hurt, or hump. I don't mean to make light. All I can say in my own defense — and I have to, don't I? — is that the thought of hurting Felice makes me sick to my stomach. I have proof that this is true: more than once in the heat of her attacks I've wrestled her down too hard, which added tears of pain onto her tears of frustration, and I have gotten sick because of it. Her responding in the affirmative to questions of my ever being violent stems from these instances and these instances alone. Again, I demand to know how these questions were asked.

As for touching her sexually, I'll just say that it simply isn't in me. I have supervised thousands of baths. She has small breasts now and some pubic hair and she has no modesty with me. I can say that I'm as aroused by an apple, or blackboard, or ocean. Let me just thank you profusely (scorn intended) for seeing your way to not manipulate the wording of your sex-abuse questions to her. Gee, seems there's one thing I haven't done wrong.

I'm almost too tired to fight you any more.

JAN 3RD

You don't answer phone messages and I need to talk. You saying Felice is "functioning well where she is" I don't buy for a second. I'm glad she's been placed in a family rather than an institution but your words "functioning well" scare the hell out of me. That's lungs, Doctor. That's digestion. That's table manners. You won't tell me what drugs you have her on because apparently I've signed away my right to know.

I'm desperate. The huge blind wheel of bureaucracy has rolled over me and left a brutal impression in the mud and it's hardening around me. I'm going to get really honest now. I'm going to let myself get loud. I hope you'll at least respect me for it and not judge me lightly. I hope there's still some reason to be talking to you.

Do you know Felice at all?

Picture a huge mountain, swarming with life. The mountain is invisible and can be seen only because of the swarm on it — not just people, and not just all the animals and insects, but all plant life too. Everything on it is moving.

At the base, things move slowly and randomly. Plants here don't grow well and are prone to fading and death. People are dazed and barely aware of their surroundings. Their state is distraction. It's a refracted sleep. They nibble at things, and their eyes go from this to that.

At middle mountain, things happen faster. There is a general energy and sense of purpose, even if it's automatic. People move more quickly because they have a destination, whether or not it's the right one. They grab for things with no doubt that this is the thing they want to grab. You can see this in their eyes. Plants do well here. (They "function well," Doctor.) Think of fields of prairie grass. Think of people at their desks and in their cars.

There are fewer people up where Felice is, not just because the top of a mountain has less room but because it's a wild and windy place and you can't stay long. Plants are at the urgent peak of bloom, a second before dying starts. People are at the tiptop height of passion — if they are having sex they are almost at orgasm. Or they are slamming the last door in a divorce, or they are about to kill someone. They are at *the verge* of spiritual enlightenment. Big-eyed foxes *an inch* from catching the rabbit. Salmon quiver as they *almost* release their eggs.

The top of Mount Appetite is the closest anything can get to heaven. It's work to get there and it's agony to be denied.

Felice is denied many times a day.

JAN 5TH

It looks like you're winning. All of you, whoever you are. My shoulders slump and I'm typing slower. In what looks suspiciously like a bid for normalcy (as if you're spying on me) I took down my Christmas lights and rooftop Santa this morning. Right on schedule, like a regulation neighbour. Santa is faded from having stood under the sun of several summers. Throughout the seasons, in moods of whup-ass fun, I've turned the lights on for birthdays — Felice's, mine, Albert Schweitzer's, Mother Theresa's, Jack Nicholson's, whoever seems worthy to my mood. Sometimes I just turn them on. I don't mind irking the neighbours. Anyone irked by a few colourful lights deserves the irk.

My other bid for normalcy, which I'll tell you about since it might make you think twice about me, is that I didn't smoke for almost a week. It wasn't hard, partly, I confess, because the world was so novel without it. Vivid and weirdly hard-assed. I felt tentative and shy, which ironically is how marijuana made me feel in the early days.

But it wasn't difficult. Again I refuse the word "addiction." I'll admit to "habit." And it's really not that bad. It makes you a little lazy. It's not as destructive as television.

Anyway, I fell off my wagon today. I don't care that you know. But delivering her box of clothes broke my heart and this was novelty I didn't need.

Naturally I want that family to fail her. It's an awful heart-split for me. Half wants Felice to be so miserable that you'll all be made to understand. The other half of course can't bear her misery. This half needs me to tell you that she'll be happiest if they choose her outfit for her the night before, and lay it out, all ready. Well, it'll not only make her happy, it'll get her to school at all. Early-morning decisions being the most violent.

Maybe they're good with her, maybe they've already figured this out. Maybe she told them, which also breaks my heart.

JAN 8TH

Probably it's good you haven't returned my calls — who knows what I'll say, and maybe there are some bridges I haven't burned yet. But I'll keep saying whatever I want.

Mount Appetite is where I live. You live here too, only you have another name for it. You call it "Desire" or something, but probably don't capitalize it, nor do you think of it as your home. I submit that you live in the state of desire at all times, even in your dreams. In Sanskrit it's called *dukkha,* or "constant dissatisfaction," which shows us a slightly different angle, a negative view of our home. I could go on and on about this mountain of ours because Felice has taught me about it for years and years and I think of it constantly — but I'll talk about it only in ways that will help your understanding of Felice.

Let me try to sum up her condition:

She knows too much. She intuits *a best.* It's not just menu items or correct spelling or which halter top. It's what they represent. Perfection. Truth. Beauty. It's within her reach. Every second. She knows she can choose perfection, at any time. She also knows she *should,* because that's the main thrust of living on this mountain. It's like the background music here, but it plays in our spine and skull. (Catholicism and its famous guilt got it right — you have to let "should" prod you heavenward at all times or you *are* damned.) Anyway, it makes us clamber, up.

Doctor, Felice can leap from the base of the mountain to the very top in one second, and it's as grotesque and startling as it's beautiful.

We know there's perfection, don't we? Come on. Can't you sense it? Isn't it right around the corner? Isn't it where that bird just went? My poor little Felice can't let go of that bird. The rest of us give up easily. We settle for the partial and the half-true, for the crumbs and shadows. Felice? She gets a whiff of the perfect and she can't not follow. She wants it, she needs it, she can't not have it. She can't let go can't let go can't let go and *she's hanging off the mountain's highest cliff with her fingernails.*

Felice can't quite find the key. She knows no one else can give it to her because they don't quite have it either. (I suffer her accusing looks.) But she's so close, she's full with it, she's raw from it. All I've been able to do is hold her, hug her hard through her violent failures.

Look at her face. Don't call me a deluded parent, because perfection *is* reflected in my daughter's face, it shines through her insane desire, you can see it coming off her like light, light that falls into my eyes as from a heaven-almost-here. She's so near the peak — foot inch millimetre — and she's grasping and she's falling and she's hitting the rocks again.

You know what I do? I watch her. Watch her and love her with gratitude for what she's showing me, love her for her sacrifice. Because in her agonies I learn myself. I see I am no different, just slicker. More adept at pretending perfection away, pretending I am not in agony myself. To watch her is to understand the mystery of the Bible — she's simply doing what Jesus did. To love her for showing me the mountain while she falls away in agony again and again — it is a love born of blood-sadness, which we all know is the only kind of love.

I wish I could watch you as you read this. I could tell where you are on this mountain. How close you are, or are not, to the top. And I could help you up. We can help each other up, even by pestering. We can also help each other off.

Because, Doctor, here's the trick. Here's what I've been on about since I sat down to give you my "version." Here's what Felice has taught me. What she has shown me, in the passion play she has performed, hourly, for years. The irony is too big for words:

Mount Appetite is futility. Mount Appetite is pettiness. Nothing is better than anything else. How can one thing be better than any other thing? How's blue better than yellow? It's impossible. *All comparisons are odious.* That's the first thing Felice teaches you. Felice can't choose what's best because there *isn't* one. In my reading I have found that Seng-T'san said it most accurately: "To set what you like against what you dislike, this is the disease of the mind."

It's not the degree of desire that is sick. The sickness is desire itself. You see this plain as day when Felice shows you the mountain, its whole height — it looms over you as the portrait of human ailment. (I think Felice sees it too. I think it's her big secret from herself.)

To see this is to be off the mountain, and be free of it, free of desire. It is wonderful — to refuse to participate. It's almost like, all along, she has been teasing me, saying, Dad! Let me show you how stupid, how futile, this struggle of ours is!

I've been a dull student. Her mother was quicker to get it, I think. Then, poof, she was gone, though I doubt there was a connection. Felice has been teaching me all this, all along, inadvertently perhaps, but perhaps not. I don't know what puts a teacher in our path.

Why tell you any of this? Maybe I still have some flicker of strategy, even though so far my sense of you is that you are a mid-mountain functionary devoid of much passion at all.

Let me try to explain another irony-that's-too-big-for-words, because you probably didn't get this one either. I desperately desire Felice back so that she can show me again in her big cartoon way that to desire anything is missing the point. I need her to come back so I can stop wanting her to come back. I need her to stop my howling. I need her to come and take my heart in both fists and pop it.

JAN 21ST — LAST NOTE TO YOU

I don't know why I pick this up again, and I have even less idea why I include you, because you've given me nothing. Maybe I still want you to understand. I also want to tell you about hope and where I just found it. Maybe I am still trying to help you up the mountain. We do need to reach the top before we can get off.

I can honestly say I have no idea where my daughter and I are as you read this. I will send it when we arrive.

Despite the restraining order I have been going to see Felice at her new school. I come at recess to watch her from the parking lot. Usually she just stands and studies the others, and this is saddening in the extreme. She already looks too tall for recess. Thankfully, this year is the last of it. Anyway, before this morning I'd never stepped out from behind the vans and cars to let her see me.

I can tell you've been giving her hard drugs. It was like she was seeing me through a filter. Please admit to yourself that they are nothing but the easiest route. Wherever we end up, I will no longer let this happen.

There is Felice, standing a timid third-of-the-way into the schoolyard. She is wearing a new wool Christmas coat that cost someone some money. That same someone had bent under pressure and allowed her to wear eyeliner. She is watching a circle of her peers, all acting cool in ways she can't, but she's getting more observant and when she practises their little ways sometimes she pulls it off. Cocking the hip, tossing the hair over the shoulder. Today, I almost don't want to interrupt her studies. But my first, smallest wave catches her attention.

She sees me and instantly can't decide what to do. She looks back to her classmates. Then over at a group of younger kids playing a bounce-ball game. She glances at the school doors, behind which is a principal, or a phone and the voice of someone like you she has been instructed to call should her father try to come get her. Then she looks back at me.

She can't decide.

And I hang by my nails from the mountain.

In fact this whole last month has had me hanging, and breathing hard. But the thing is, Felice decided. Sometimes it's possible to see the truth and grab it, running.

ACKNOWLEDGEMENTS

Many of the stories in this collection were first published in magazines, periodicals or anthologies: "The Alcoholist" in *Event*, and *Best Canadian Stories, '01* (Oberon); "Maria's Older Brother" in *The Fiddlehead*, and *Deep Cove Stories* (Oolichan); "The Little Addict That Could" in *The Malahat Review*; "Driving Under the Influence" in *Exile*; "Where It Comes From, Where It Goes" (winner of the CBC Canadian Literary Award) in *Saturday Night* and *The Shambhala Sun*; "The Northern Cod" in *Grain*, and *Entering the Landscape* (Oberon); "Mount Appetite" in *The Malahat Review*; "Comedian Tire" in *Prism International*; "The Angels' Share" in *Event*; "The Bronze Miracle" in *The Malahat Review*, and *Deep Cove Stories* (Oolichan); "Forest Path" (previously as "The Forest Path to Malcolm's") in *Canadian Fiction Magazine*, and *Deep Cove Stories* (Oolichan). The author wishes to thank the editors. And cheers to my agent Carolyn Swayze.

*B*ILL GASTON GREW UP IN Winnipeg, Toronto and North Vancouver. Aside from teaching at various universities, he has worked as a logger, salmon fishing guide, group home worker and, most exotically, a hockey player in the south of France. Gaston has published four acclaimed novels, one of which, *The Good Body,* was recently released by HarperCollins in the US. He has also published three previous, stellar short story collections, including the much-praised *Sex is Red* (1999), produced plays and written for television. In 1999, he won the CBC/Saturday Night Canadian Literary Award for fiction.

Bill Gaston lives in Victoria, British Columbia, where he teaches at the University of Victoria.

MORE FINE FICTION FROM RAINCOAST AND POLESTAR

A Reckless Moon and Other Stories • by Dianne Warren
A beautifully written book about human fragility, endorsed by Bonnie Burnard. "Warren is clearly one of a new generation of short-story writers who have learned their craft in the wake of such luminaries as Raymond Carver and Ann Beattie ... Her prose is lucid and precise."
— *Books in Canada*
1-55192-455-2 • $21.95 CAN / $15.95 USA

A Sack of Teeth • by Grant Buday
This darkly humorous novel paints an unforgettable portrait of one extraordinary day in the life of a father, a mother and a six-year-old child in September 1965. "Buday's genius is that of the storyteller."
— *Vancouver Sun*
1-55192-457-9 • $21.95 CAN / $15.95 USA

Small Accidents • by Andrew Gray
Twelve dazzling stories by a Journey Prize finalist. "Andrew Gray tells tall tales that tap into the hubris of the human condition ... He expertly depicts the gore of human error and conveys a present as startling as a car wreck."
— Hal Niedzviecki
1-55192-508-7 • $19.95 CAN / $14.95 USA

Pool-Hopping and Other Stories • by Anne Fleming
Shortlisted for the Governor-General's Award, the Ethel Wilson Fiction Prize and the Danuta Gleed Award. "Fleming's evenhanded, sharp-eyed and often hilarious narratives traverse the frenzied chaos of urban life with ease and precision."
— *The Georgia Straight*
1-896095-18-6 • $16.95 CAN / $13.95 USA

What's Left Us • by Aislinn Hunter
Six stories and an unforgettable novella by a prodigiously talented writer. "Aislinn Hunter is a gifted writer with a fresh energetic voice and a sharp eye for the detail that draws you irresistibly into the intimacies of her story."
— Jack Hodgins
1-55192-412-9 • $21.95 CAN / $15.95 USA